Slavery and Salvation

Slavery and Salvation

Alastair Redfern

ISPCK

2020

Slavery and Salvation - Published by the Indian Society for Promoting Christian Knowledge (ISPCK), Post Box 1585, Kashmere Gate, Delhi-110006.

ISBN: 978-93-88945-60-8

Cover Picture Credit: Internet Sources

Laser typeset by

ISPCK, Post Box 1585, 1654, Madarsa Road, Kashmere Gate, Delhi-110006 • *Tel:* 23866323

e-mail: ashish@ispck.org.in • ella@ispck.org.in
website: www.ispck.org.in

Printed at Saurabh Printers, NOIDA.

Contents

Preface ... vii

Introduction ... ix

PART ONE
Slavery and Salvation: Christian Foundations

Chapter - 1
The Shaping of Scripture and Tradition ... 3

PART TWO
Contemporary Challenges

Chapter - 2
Choice – The Formation of Discipleship ... 17

Chapter - 3
Demand and Desire ... 28

Chapter - 4
Morality ... 41

PART THREE
Power and Powerlessness

Chapter - 5

Victims and Justice   ... 53

Chapter - 6

Sovereignty and Lordship   ... 64

PART FOUR
Gospel Resources

Chapter - 7

The Slave who Serves the Master   ... 75

Chapter - 8

St Paul and the New Household of Faith   ... 89

Chapter - 9

Slavery – The Ecclesial Vocation: An Anglican Response   ... 100

PART FIVE
Discipleship and Mission

Chapter - 10

The Spirituality of The Slave Disciple   ... 113

Epilogue

Romans 6:16-22

Galatians 5:13-14   ... 123

Preface

As I have become more deeply involved in the fight against Modern Slavery, I have been challenged to reflect upon the particular contribution of the Christian faith – always to be offered alongside the work of a huge range of partners. This small book is an attempt to share some reflections upon a few of the key themes – within the Christian faith, and within contemporary society and the forces enabling slavery to flourish.

The aim is to encourage a deeper mining of the resources entrusted to the church, and a recognition of our tendency to limit their missionary and saving powers by confining them to set forms and frameworks. The challenge of Modern Slavery is a call to re-explore the significant fact that the Gospel operates through the coming of the Kingdom which is good news for all, and especially for the un-noticed and the oppressed. The tendency to create ecclesial responses to this gift of grace which focus upon what has been received, rather than taking the key agenda from the continuing story of the Passion in human living, always need checking and refocusing.

My involvement in the fight against Modern Slavery has challenged me to go back to the Fount and Framer of Christian faith once again. I hope others may be similarly challenged.

Introduction

These essays represent an attempt to explore the phenomenon of Modern Slavery from a number of angles – including those of Christian belief and practice, forces in contemporary society, revelation from the underside of our unfolding human story, and the dynamics of power, both exercised from above and as expressed in self sacrificial service from below.

As the systems we inevitably construct to better order human living are always in need of refinement, not least in terms of enabling greater inclusivity and equality, so the values that encourage us to support and develop them need to be explored against the widest criteria that can help us recognise the central importance of the well-being of people and of the planet.

My work with the Clewer Initiative and with the Global Sustainability Network provides both the material and the reflections which inform the exploration of these themes. Part One recognises that the key is an examination of Christian foundations in relation to the whole challenge of Modern Slavery, and the nuances which extend an appreciation of both culpability and the possibility of effective response.

The second section highlights some of the factors and forces in a current situation which encourage both the growth of slavery, and the silent complicity in so many citizens and consumers. The issues of choice, demand/desire and morality: the web of values and practices which drive exploitation and exclusion while providing satisfactions for so many consumers – so that the deeper links between the oppression of some and the pursuit of freedom by others, is scarcely noticed, let alone addressed. Modern Slavery provides the touchstone of this prevalent and deeply destructive process.

The third section seeks to examine the role of "victims", and the dynamics of power, from above and from below, that not only enable the problem, but also provide the seeds of a robust and effective response. A way of life and a set of values that can bring hope to people and the planet.

The next section explores the practical resources of the Christian tradition to identify and to deliver models of such newness of life and saving inclusivity.

A final chapter invites reflection upon the calling to be a disciple given this context, challenge and call to respond creatively. The implications for Christian mission come to the fore.

These materials represent a call for Christians, churches and people of goodwill to consider the nature of the challenges posed by Modern Slavery and how we can play an effective role in helping to craft a positive and life-saving response – for all of us.

A much more detailed account of the workings of Modern Slavery, and the practical responses possible, is provided in my book 'The Clewer Initiative'.[1]

The aim of these chapters is to provoke action and reflection – not to provide answers. A living and very sophisticated crime requires a living and flexible response. I hope that some of these materials might enable an appreciation, development, correction and critique, that issues in a deeper seeing of this hidden oppression, and a stronger response in terms of recognition, rescue, restoration and the reframing of values and practices accordingly.

Slavery involves us all – the call and the challenge is how to discern an appropriate response, including a recognition of how best the various contributions can fit together in the service of the different 'Households' in which we live.

Endnotes

[1] Alastair Redfern. *The Clewer Initiative*. ISPCK 2017.

PART ONE

Slavery and Salvation: Christian Foundations

CHAPTER - 1

The Shaping of
Scripture and Tradition

Being a Slave

'Slave' is a term and an identity often used in the New Testament, especially by Jesus with regard to His own identity, and in highlighting moments of judgement and the need for decision – echoing an Old Testament approach whereby to be part of the enslaved was a distinctive mark in the sight of God: a sign of receiving a special vocation.

This is one model of human being. A Creator who is Lord and Master, and the dependency of all creatures upon this 'One'. However, there is a temptation to make provision for the self or the group, and ignore this basic commonness, which creates division and exploitation among human beings, and distance from the purposes of God for all His children to be part of a single, coming kingdom.

Thus, there is a second, more worldly understanding of slavery, focused on the differing agendas of master and slave, of the powerful and the powerless.

The teaching and example of Jesus does not simply promote the first model of one Creator and a proper dependent slavery of all creatures to His purposes, at the expense of denying or denigrating the second model, which emerges in systems and relationships of oppression and inclusion. Rather, Jesus seems to invite His followers to work within the human model of master-slave: though with a different spirit and a more constructive agenda that will begin to transform systems and relationships – not to create some kind of equality, but to encourage a willing acceptance of a call to slavery to God and to others, as the way to fulfil self, complete God's calling and to become one with Christ through sharing in His sacrificial service.

As St Paul tells the Galatians:

"For you were called into freedom: only do not use your freedom as an opportunity for self-indulgence, but through love become slaves to one another. For the whole law is summed up in a single commandment: you shall love your neighbour as yourself." (Galatians 5:13—14).

This form of godly slavery is fulfilled by living the fruit of the spirit – love, joy, peace, patience, kindness, generosity, faithfulness, gentleness and self-control. All ways of denying the immediate satisfaction of the self in order to be more fully a slave to God and to others. Such slaves will be given an appropriate allowance (Matthew 24:45—end) and will experience the Master coming to serve them (Luke 12:37; John 13:1—20).

A Slave in A Household

Thus, to be a slave to Christ the Lord was not a separated calling. In John 4:43, when the son of the Royal official is healed, this is reported to him on his homeward journey by his slaves, so "he himself believed along with his whole household". Slavery was a calling for a whole range of roles in the Household, and the essential disposition of all Christians one towards another. Thus Paul, on four occasions, proclaims himself to be a "slave" of Christ (Romans 1:1; Galatians 1:1; Philippians 1:1; Titus 1:1) as part of a calling to be a "slave of all" (1 Corinthians 9:19). This presents a radical challenge to the Western liberal model of freedom being defined by the qualities of being unique and autonomous, and facing the stress of ever negotiating appropriate roles and relationships from this very subjective perspective and identity.

The challenge of this strange vocation included resisting the temptation which Paul explores in Romans 6 and 7 of becoming enslaved to sin (echoing our Lord's own words in John 8:32), which involves succumbing to the ever present temptation to put the self at the centre, rather than simply being part of the life of the Body or the Household. In 1 Timothy it is clear that the church embraced a vast range of people: rich women (2:9—10), the wealthy (6:17—19), widows – rich, poor, young, elderly (5:3—16), those who wanted to be rich (6:1—2), patrons who owned slaves (6:1—2), slaves (6:1—2), and those of different theological positions (1:3—4; 4:13; 6:3—5, 20—24).

The Traditional Household Economy

The key connector and adjudicator for all these types of people within the established norms of that society was seen as 'the love of money' which became the root of all evil (6:10). The distribution and stewardship of money was the prime indicator of the distribution of power and the unfolding of status. Thus the first stage for the leaven of the Christian gospel is mutual respect and service – focused in the common prayer and the sharing of the bread. Jesus, Paul, and their contemporaries were not operating in a culture of 'rights' where a key lever to change would be reformulating laws. Pharasaic and Roman law were 'givens', overseen through powerful and well defended hierarchies – the defences being both physical and cultural. Both Jesus and Paul therefore look to the fulfilling of the law of love by a concentration upon its true foundations (love of God and love of neighbour as oneself), and through the leaven and enlightening of practice within existing structures and legal framing that would have the effect of transforming future practice and perception. A process of development through the deconstruction of current views and values – to enable the evolving of new and more inclusive perspectives and practices. Not simply the reflective dialectic associated with Hegel as a philosophical enterprise, but more in tune with the sometimes-neglected Hegelian insight that this creative process of fracture and the facing of limitation unfolds by means of a common spirit operating through suffering towards redemption. There will be a continuing cost to this calling to own the limitations of practices which seemed secure, comfortable and 'natural'.

A New Dynamic – Learning Godliness

As Hegel wrote in his Encyclopaedia Logic:

> "The aim of the Master – slave dialectic is to show that we cannot view ourselves as pure, unique particulars, and to show that we must come to an awareness of others as selves in their own right, by recognising that we all share a common universal essence......"[1]

The key is not dogma (which tends to enshrine limitation and create boundaries) – but what Hegel terms 'idealism'. This is the ground of what Jesus calls the potential of seeds, light, salt or leaven. Change from within existing structures and systems, to enable the often-mysterious growth of richer fruitfulness. This is why the Gospel, in Jesus, in Paul, in the Early Church, is about testimony – the witness of new values being put into practice through service of others rather than through great schemes and ideologies.

In 1 Timothy 6:17—19, the rich, and those who aspire to be rich (the choice for mammon as a tool for putting self at the centre), are told not to "set hopes on the uncertainty of riches, but rather on God who richly provides us (i.e. the Christian community in all its diversity) with every blessing for our enjoyment." The key to gospel witness is to do good, to be generous and ready to share – so that the understandable concern for 'self' is focused upon the treasure of a good foundation for the future of the Body of Christ as the agent of the Kingdom of God. To "take hold of the life that is really life." A new approach to investment, within the apparent clarity of a political, social and religious culture which uniformly demoted slaves, women and heathens to places of vulnerable dependence upon the power of others.

Salvation involved a training in godliness (1 Timothy 4:8) within the voluntary association of the ecclesia.

An interesting parallel to this approach can be found in the Stoic philosophy of Seneca, an almost exact contemporary of St Paul:

> "They are slaves you urge: no, they are men
> They are slaves: no, they are comrades
> They are slaves: no, they are humble friends
> They are slaves: no they are fellow slaves, if you reflect that fortune
> has the same power over both.
> Let some of them dine with you, because they are worthy."[2]

James Fitton, writing amidst the struggles around slavery in America in 1863 identified the church as "not just a great and fruitful school, but a regenerative association."[3] Thus Christian witness and gospel direction was unfolded through the force of ideas (in one spirit were we all baptised: 1 Corinthians 12:13), being incarnated, or put into practice. The mutual recognition and service of slaves and Masters (Ephesians 6:5—9; Colossians 3:24—25) as a first step in improving the actual working environment of slaves; and the care and nourishment of freed slaves. A process of reflection, practice and the offering of new models and images.

Of course this strategy, while realistic in a very different culture in terms of power, role and change, did allow the continuation of what could be a brutalising and inhumane system. A tragic and challenging example would be the later growth of the transatlantic slave trade and the huge effect in terms of racism and oppression, based on appeals to biblical teaching.

Prophecy

Thus the crucial role of prophecy to crystalize calls for the consideration of more radical, and therefore effective, values and practices. For example in an Easter sermon in 379 Gregory of Nyssa called this festival the feast of liberation and warned that no one could put a price on God's image, insisting that slavery existed as the law of the Devil, contrary to the Creators law.

But, as religion has become dispersed in a marketplace of values and choices, the role of business in the ordering of desire within the frame of mammon has become predominant. Governments are retreating from the detailed responsibilities of a welfare state model, and struggling even to provide viable common frameworks for a civil society. In fact civil society has become more clearly the market economy of autonomous individuals which Hegel had recognised – trivialising lifestyles and commodifying human relations.

The prophetic voice asking for and modelling the inclusion of the vulnerable and the enslaved has no ready place in which to be proclaimed or enacted – faced by a bewildering plethora of social media spaces and competing pressure groups. Prophecy becomes domesticated, and is rarely able to be heard outside of preselected echo chambers.

The challenge for a Christian witness is how to move from universal values being pronounced but largely ignored, into a more modest and tactically complex role of joining in the flow of goodness. Shifting from comprehensive statements and policies, towards acts of annunciation – evoking insights and actions that enable the accessing of grace. This represents almost a full turn of the circle, to the New Testament context of seeking to offer leaven and light into a 'disconnected' and mammon focused web of cultures and tribes. The progression towards institutional and teaching coherence, articulated through policy statements which could be traced from Gregory of Nyssa to the World Council of Churches has to be recognised as a seductive model whose strengths are increasingly inadequate for the task at hand. Not least the challenge of Modern Slavery to government, business, faith, academia, community groups and the emergence of popular philanthropy.

As a result, there is a temptation for Christian energy to adopt the approach of the therapeutic world – pastoral care, often in the form of some kind of chaplaincy. But these disciplines tend to privilege the self and have struggled to engage creatively with the institutional and the corporate arrangements which already exist, and which cooperate to permit the continuing exploitation and exclusion of the vulnerable.

Prophecy provides the challenging frame for the pastoral outworking of faith in a common future and fulfilment. The urgent task for those who aspire to hold and inhabit such faith is to discern better how to make salt which is sharper, and not easily lost in the midst of all the more obvious ingredients that people seek to contribute to the increasingly exotic mix that characterises contemporary participative society. Salt, leaven, light, seeds, need to be prepared carefully and aimed strategically into the noisy kaleidoscope of modern living. So that unjust and oppressive practices can be better exposed. Hence the strapline of the Clewer Initiative as a church response to Modern Slavery: "we see you."[4] Such a statement can only be properly prophetic if it brings accurate diagnosis and assessment of the expanding phenomenon of human vulnerability, while also offering signposts towards more wholesome and viable alternatives. Deconstruction and development through a richer indwelling of the Spirit who inhabits each creature, and ever seeks to open the individual and the particular into the personal of expanded relationships, and the universal of greater inclusivity in the well-being of society.

The Gospel Strategy

The use of the model of 'slavery' in the New Testament is a prophetic strategy that begins with what seems like the most fixed and weak element of social and economic relationships, enshrined in contemporary philosophy and religious practices. From such an unlikely and untried source comes the model of the Messiah and the source of salvation – not just for economic slaves, but for all who live by being enslaved to limited and excluding values and practices. The model of slavery becomes a common calling that not only has the potential to undermine the myriad Master – slave relationships which seem to provide shortcuts to human security and role identity, by creating various forms of slavery, but also brings power to perceive and engage with a fuller way of expressing and organising human living together.

This is the 'way' enfleshed in the life, death and resurrection into glory of Jesus Christ. The dynamic of discipleship developed by St Paul and the first Christian witnesses to this good news for all. The following chapters explore possible ways of interpreting such a prophetic witness and highlight lessons which might be learned for our own response in a world within which boundaries between people seem to be hardening both politically, in the form of new tribalism and populisms, and socially, with the creation of self-affirming 'echo chambers' through Facebook pages and Twitter accounts. Slavery, in terms of the commodification, exclusion and exploitation of others, is becoming an increasingly inevitable outcome of how these narrowly 'personal' expressions of self are encouraged to unfold within the atomising forces of the market – which creates illusions of commonness and connectivity through moments of fashion, while in fact keeping people focused on self and indifferent to the well-being or inclusion of others.

Prophecy is always a call to richer participation – in aspiration as in action. The challenge is to discern and develop appropriate models and metaphors.

The Slave And The Lamb

For the Christian Gospel there are two key metaphors. Jesus chose to call Himself a slave. Others called Him the Lamb of God, come to take away the sins of the world. Both a slave and a lamb are figures with no self agency: totally controlled by others, and dependent upon agendas not related to their own aspirations or desires.

The deeply challenging tradition of calling the first to be last, and to seek the lowest place, to act as a slave rather than a Master – points toward the Gospel paradox that it is only through the powerlessness of utter commitment to the needs of the other, that real purpose and agency can be discerned. Much of the teaching and example of Jesus involve reaching across the established boundaries of control and exclusion, to invite the unnoticed and the excluded to participate – to join in a fuller fellowship – often around the sharing of food and the possibility of those previously separated by lifestyles and conventions being able to become friends.

This is, of course, the dynamic of Christian worship – the sharing of food and friendship to embrace any who will participate, regardless of role, status or resources (or their absence). The key measure and ingredient of this radically inclusive gathering is the presence of the Lamb, the slave, of the excluded and ignored and oppressed.

Here is a metaphor and a methodology for recognising the worldly realities that continually create Modern Slavery, and for identifying how the good news of salvation for all might be crafted and communicated.

Endnotes
[1] G.W.F. Hegel. *Encyclopaedia of the Philosophical Sciences. Part One (1830)*. Translated by William Wallace. OUP. 1975, P52-53

[2] Letter 47 to Lucilius. See K. Vogt. Seneca. Stanford U.P. 2007, p282

[3] J. Fitton. *Influence of Catholic Christian Doctrines on the Emancipation of Slaves*. Palala Press. 2018, p1

[4] The Clewer Initiative.org

Questions For Further Reflection
And Group Discussion

1. Paul proclaims himself to be "a slave of Christ", as part of the calling to be "a slave of all". How might this kind of vocation be understood in an age of human rights?

2. What do you understand by "a common spirit operating through suffering towards redemption"?

3. "Prophecy becomes domesticated and is rarely able to be heard outside of preselected echo chambers". How might the challenge of the Christian gospel be heard beyond the pastoral witness of the church?

4. Can the image of the Slave and the Lamb still be used effectively today? If so, how?

PART TWO
Contemporary Challenges

CHAPTER - 2

Choice –
The Formation of Discipleship

Pietism and Personal Growth

Morality can be understood as the framework within which to share human desire. In modern times desire operates increasingly through individual choice – and morality becomes the attempt to maximise the possibilities of such choice within a publicly acceptable framework. The result can be that Christian justice and our understanding of the meaning of choice translates into a sense of responsibility through which the Christian, as an individual, expresses this faith by choosing to be charitable. Sometime this generosity is aggregated by combining with others – in what might be called the 'Christian aid' approach.

In this plausible way, God's call to be disciples for the sake of the world becomes reduced to a refraction through which individuals craft a highly personalised response. Then the driver for appropriate discipleship becomes the attempt to improve the quality of each individual journey. As a result Christians are called conscientiously to try to measure and improve performance. The self becomes the measure, rather than sacrificial concern about the kind of corporate categories which Jesus employed in the Gospels: "the poor, the sick, the hungry, the thirsty, the blind...." (Luke 4; Matthew 25). Such an approach to discipleship brings an emphasis upon a spirituality of 'pietism and personal growth'.[1]

Partnership and Participation

In fact the real Gospel call is not focused upon "my faith in Jesus", but always the emphasis is about my being drawn into the faith of Jesus. This is made clear in Jesus telling His disciples "I now call your friends", or Paul choosing the word 'apostles'. This highlights the importance of the institutional arrangements of Christianity, which provide a frame within which to discern and express the choice to participate in coordinated callings and contributions to society – most dramatically portrayed in the sharing of a common life in Acts 2 and 4.

For these reasons the Fellowship or ecclesia has choices to make. Underlying this Gospel insight is the recognition of the priority of God's choice, "when I consider the heavens, the work of your hands.... The moon and the stars .... then I say what is man that you are mindful of him? Yet you have made him a little lower than God, and crowned him with glory and honour... And put all things in subjection under his feet?" (Psalm 8:3—6).

Here is a calling from insignificance within the vast mysteries of creation, to oversight and stewardship of creation, through the empowering of humanity to contribute to the unfolding of the creativity which ever advances fulfilment. Thus each individual is always part of the calling of humanity to work towards the salvation of the world.

This spirit within human being is the spirit of Trinity – the dynamic Creator, Redeemer, Sustainer, providing a frame for choosing in a way that can become aligned with and part of God's choice. In the complexity of a fallen world, manifested through the classic tensions and differentiations between master/slave: Jew/Greek: male/female (Galatians 3:28), the human contribution is modelled by the image of the slave – washing feet and noticing the needy in ways which unfold through appropriate response. Such choice directly contradicts and confronts the self-centred choices which individuals and more narrowly focused groups tend to make. Instead, there is choice to cooperate with the coming of a Kingdom.

The sign of The Cross

Choices for a new sociability need to be based upon a desire to give rather than the desire to receive – thus suggesting the possibility of radically different structures and relationships. To enable this life-giving transition, desire should be washed in baptism and expressed through participation in a common meal at which the One Lord and Master presided. His supper becomes the sign or sacrament which is constitutive of Paul's development of the Household, the Christian gathering for nourishment and guidance.

The power and reference point for such choice – by God, and by human response – is the cross of Christ – a particular way of Messiah-ship that is leadership into the promised land.

"I, if I be lifted up, will draw all men to myself". This is God's choice, to offer, model, invite – so that human choice might learn to walk in this way of the cross – through which darkness becomes light, and struggling life becomes eternal love. Such choices call God and humankind into an including covenant (Mark 14:25). This expresses the Spirit of the High Priestly prayer in John 17 – that they all may be one, i.e. that all may choose to respond in this way to this sign of the cross.

Waiting and Working for the Kingdom

Of course in practice, choice is always complex in the human environment. A good example would be the parable of the labourers in the vineyard (Matthew 20: 1—16). All who choose to make themselves available in the marketplace for God's call/ invitation are welcome. But the choice to be open to this call and offer is specific in its response to, and trust in, a certain calling and acceptance of delegated roles.

The discernment of such a calling requires patience to wait, pay attention, and be glad to receive such an invitation. The sense of need to maintain and develop the self and one's core group, easily takes precedence. Succumbing to such a temptation many enter the marketplace and march directly into the vineyard of the world's workings, to create transactions and systems for their own immediate welfare, often in competition with others. The purpose is flourishing for self and for immediate satisfactions.

Some engage for more limited outcomes such as short-term gains, easily measurable, on their own terms. Yet some within the place of the market are willing to make themselves available, in faith, for the larger purposes of creation. They wait, listen, and connect to the possibilities of such a choice at different stages of the day of their life. Yet all who are willing to wait and be called, faithful in their patience and persistence, even up to the last minute, can participate. It is in the mystery of God's choice that people are invited to work on the kingdom project – the managing of the vineyard – and the challenge is to remain attentive to receiving the invitation. There are many tasks and therefore choices to cultivate both temporal and eternal fruits. The complexity is the interplay between these two ways of making choices, not least because there remains the necessity for systems and structures to enable and handle the making of choices.

At one level this is still, in its most immediate sense, an earthly agenda of food for survival, nourishment and pleasure. Yet the context can become a new community where choices are made to be joined in a common overall enterprise under the leadership of one Head: one Master. This represents a different kind of social integration, for common outcomes, all within a spirit of radical generosity and the acceptance of the inevitability of different responses and attitudes.

In this model choice is not about an individual deciding to contribute simply for their own well-being, nor is it about a church seeking to facilitate that kind of personally positive and measurable outcome. Rather, in this context, choice means the recognition of God's call and invitation, via the Cross of suffering, uncertainty, waiting, and through the subsequent human response to a Fellowship through which the Master creates a new community bonded in the gift of His generosity towards all – a microcosm of the vineyard which heralds His coming kingdom.

The marketisation and mobilisation of tasks, roles and relationships means that choices have become more confined and individualised. There is a consequent tendency for church to become an individual choice through which that person can then decide to be generous to others. By contrast, prophetic witness invites us to try to recover a sense of a Christian calling to be part of an intentional working community, forwarding the agenda of the vineyard – a choice to become part of the working Household of the Father, embraced in His generosity, and choosing to assist or serve in enabling such grace to be made available to others, who languish in vulnerability and uncertainty often outside of the normal workings of the marketplace. The generosity of the Master is shared through the sacrificial service of His workers, His slaves, in particular places or contexts, so that others can be rescued from exclusion.

Commonwealths of Committed Service
Because Christians have become individualised as citizens, with individual votes, and as consumers, with individual choice, there is a prophetic need to more proactively and self-consciously establish commonwealths as models and contributors to wider social welfare and more inclusive human flourishing. Choice thus becomes the key expression of the agenda of the Household – as Paul made clear with regard to food and belief. The key is the Masters including generosity, not our petty excluding short term schemes.

The transcending power to inform and connect all choice is morality as understood by the church, so that politics – that is the working out of choice – is given a soul. Thus in Ephesians 4: 9 there are many callings but 'all for the building up of the body of Christ'. Again in St John 'except a grain of wheat falls into the ground and dies, it remains a single grain: if it dies, it brings forth much fruit' (John 12:24).

Choice therefore in a Christian sense is the means for the renewal of the mind (in Christ). As St Paul makes clear in Romans 12:2, this renewal is not about knowledge, nor in 1 Corinthians 1: 18—25 is it about self-consciousness. Rather renewal through the ecclesia is about being enabled to relate to the project of the Messiah – whereby a slave in the midst of slavery chooses to reinforce this particular role and calling – the kind of choice dramatically enacted in the Garden of Gethsemane when Jesus confirms His calling: not my will but thy will be done (Luke 22:42). In Romans 13:4, Paul provides a list of little groups of mainly oppressed persons who have joined his Messianic assemblies and become the vanguards of the sons and daughters of God. A point reinforced in Romans 8. All sorts and conditions of people are called and commissioned for work in the vineyard.

For Paul, the law has a key role in providing shaping for the choices which human beings are invited to make, so as to best conform to God's ways of working. In this sense choice is partly expressed through the law – which is fulfilled in one command: "You shall love your neighbour as yourself". Throughout the New Testament the revelation in Jesus Christ is an extended uncovering of who is my neighbour, and of ways of enfleshing the love which God chooses to pour out appropriately to His vulnerable children trapped in the marketplace with little proper sustenance or security.

Kenosis and Klesis

The theological word for such choice is kenosis – meaning to prioritise the needs of the nearest embodiment of the Messiah highlighted in vulnerable human flesh, and then to pursue the signs and measures He has enacted in order for such mercy to be put into practice. Thus kenosis enables an exodus from enslavement to the self so as to allow the disciple to contribute to the community sharing God's love. Such choice emerges not from knowledge of self – the trajectory of some strands of contemporary spirituality – but rather from the awakening of connection to the Messianic event – that is to choose to be part of a presence most manifest in human need, and which is always heavily pregnant with the possibility of practical outcomes for greater wholeness.

In this way choice becomes the inhabiting of the generous calling and gifting of the Master. Klesis (calling) emerges as kenosis (slave like self-giving), leading to identification and solidarity with the vulnerable. This is the point St Paul is making in Galatians 2:19—20 when he states, "I have been crucified with the Messiah – it is no longer I who live…" or again "rather to live is to be baptised into Christ death" (Romans 6:3—4). And in 2 Corinthians 4:10—11 "We always carry about in the body the death of Jesus".

Therefore the choice of God calls us to choose death of self – but this is never negative as in the world's understanding of death. In 2 Corinthians 5:15 Paul makes clear that "He died for all, so that those who live might live no longer for themselves, but for Him who for their sakes died and was raised". His choice invites our choice – to be manifested in concrete behaviour (Romans 13:13—14). A powerful example is Paul's collection for the poor, since the vulnerable are always the touchstone. This was a radically practical choice since "he who loves the other has fulfilled the law".

Greek and Roman society assumed that true love depended upon sameness, affinity, familiarity – very similar to the homogenising effects of our contemporary market economy. And yet Paul's assemblies (Households) were always open to the other – to those who were different, asymmetrical, unfamiliar, potentially threatening. Moreover, because the ecclesia was not a collective, but a singular subject in Christ, all were united in a deeper identity through a common Messianic choice and loyalty to the event of the cross as the key to enabling a common salvation. Thus in Romans 12:5 "we are members of one another" that is, to be Christian is to choose to give up individual choice and accept the discipline to discern God's choice, unfolding in particular contexts that we need to proactively discern and respond to with generosity – since " one died for all " (2 Corinthians 5:14; Romans 5:6—8).

In similar vein, to a mixed, open group gathering, Paul advises "welcome one another as Christ welcomed you, for the glory of God" (Romans 15:7).

God and Mammon

This call to exercise choice by placing oneself in the service of another – of Jesus the Lord – has been obscured by the post-Enlightenment liberal project of promoting freedom and toleration, through the mechanism of individual rights and voting powers. The dynamic has moved from individuals who might more willingly contribute to the social, communal contexts in which they find themselves, to a market-driven impetus toward the prioritisation of personal values and experiences so that choices are focused upon individuals perceived needs and tastes. This privatisation of choice increases the focus upon wealth, the gap between rich and poor, and shines attention upon the have's (whose needs define the market in goods and also our understanding of values and ideas) and divert public and personal vision away from the have-nots – who are not just excluded but ignored, unseen and unheard.

Christian discipleship understood as personal conversion and formation produces a dangerous conformity to this market environment and is subtly reinforced by the genuine call to charity. The problem of exclusion, growing vulnerability and modern slavery is therefore exacerbated. Choice focused upon individual beliefs, behaviour and lifestyle- values creates the sense of personal calling and goodwill which allows our apparently mature civilisation, based upon individual rights, to in fact be a society in which the seduction of choice creates the space for the evils of criminal exploitation and oppression of those too vulnerable and unfortunate to be able to claim their rights or grow their own self-centred resources.

This dilemma is at the heart of our Lord's teaching about the choice between God and mammon. The latter represents wealth accumulated for the self, for worldly concerns and benefits – the way of the rich young ruler, or the parable of Dives and Lazarus. The marks of apparently successful choice in worldly terms create a blindness to the needs of others made equally in the image of God – a blindness that leads to judgement if eyes cannot be opened. This was the agenda of Jesus's engagement with the Pharisees.

Choice is between alternative perspectives – either such narrow vision that only the self and its needs or satisfactions can be seen, or the wider perspective that notices, appreciate and connects with the desires of others – these represent the choice between God and Mammon.

And such a perspective is not easily maintained. It is not a simple or one-off choice. This is the message that we can discern from the behaviour of the crowds in Holy Week. One moment there is acclamation for Jesus as Lord, strewing His way with cloaks and palms. The next day the shout is "crucify" – that is give Him the death of a slave.

Choice is the continuing condition of a human being. God and Mammon represent the options. The way of discipleship conceived through the signs of the slave, and of the Lamb, are the indicators that provide the formation which strengthens resistance to choosing self and risks choosing the service of the other.

Endnotes

[1] F. R. Barry. *St Paul and Social Psychology.* OUP 1922, p4.

Questions For Further Reflection And Group Discussion

1. Read the parable of the Labourers in the Vineyard in Matthew 20:1—16. The invitation is a vocation or calling to serve the Master, and His generosity, alongside others. How does this approach compare to contemporary approaches to vocation?

2. How might we respond to a call to Exodus from enslavement to self? What might this involve?

3. What might be involved for us in choosing between God and mammon?

4. How can our personal choice be committed to prioritising the needs of others?

CHAPTER - 3

Demand and Desire

Slavery to Self

Modern Slavery is driven by demand – for services, low costs, power relationships beyond normal conventions of balance or mutuality – a focused, person centred energy for fulfilment in a certain frame. The development of consumerism as the key driver to the market has become centred around the provoking of insatiable demand. Hence the power of fashion. The public relations industry also aims to create desire for persons, products, images and experiences.

The response of Christian teaching in the face of this shift from a society based upon laws which presumed set places and order, reinforced by religious and social convention, to a constant call to imagine and satisfy 'desires' for each self, has been to focus upon pastoral care and support. Attempts to provide frameworks of control and prohibition in terms of the individualised drivers of the market have been largely abandoned.

Thus the market offers desire for momentary satisfaction, often closely allied to sexual images, aspirations and experiences. Desire for mutuality has been swept away by desire as fulfilment for stimulated wants and needs. And when stress or casualties occur, the role of Christian faith is to supplement the therapy industry – putting the individual at the centre and helping that person best handle 'their' desires. There is little emphasis upon giving the self away into the needs of others and for the sake of the community. Instead counselling and some approaches to spirituality tend to reinforce the individual as needing to be in control – anything but a 'slave', when in fact slavery to self has become the standard form of identity.

Therefore demand is an expression of human desire – which the modern market environment cultivates and concentrates upon as 'event': a moment of purchase, of pleasure, of possession. An event or moment providing an excess of satisfaction above the normal expectation of the public, every day way of living.

Slave Services
Modern Slave slavery highlights this feature of the market – by providing human agents to enable the event of 'excess', of super satisfaction:

1. Forced labour – very low-cost goods and services providing deals too good to be true.

2. Sexual exploitation – sexual encounter totally tailored to the purchasers self-perceived needs, fantasies and power demands.

3. Organ trafficking – a life changing event, of improvement for the recipient, of dimunition for the coerced donor.

4. Forced marriage – a life event perpetuating asymmetrical power and practical arrangements.

5. Begging – each coin in the pot feeds a criminal gang and reinforces the marginality of the beggar.

6. Domestic servitude – zero cost home services.

7. County lines – drug sales events that feed addiction and entrap the dependency of the seller by reinforcing the power dominance of the trader.

8. Orphanages – have also become an expanding business – an excess of control of kidnapped and dubiously acquired children enables the encouragement of an excessive charity from the West.

The market hones the sophistication of these kind of 'events' to give a taste of excess satisfaction to the purchaser or beneficiary through the dimunition and disempowerment of the human agent providing the experience or service.

Mauss, in his classic work on the gift recognises that exchange is never just financial but is always also personal.[1] With modern slavery one person is magnified: the other is diminished. This reality is used by the market but hidden by its public presentation as a financial transaction chosen by the purchaser and supposedly beneficial to the supplier by providing work and income. In fact this dynamic is the offering of the services that feeds desire and keeps it hungry for more, with no thought for the provider.

Disciplining Desire

This contrasts strongly with Christian wisdom about the importance of discipline and of limits to desire – for the good of self and for the good of society. Those who are called into this community of the Master's generosity, need to reflect upon this contrast and learn to see the market through the eyes of its victims. This will enable a recognition of a deeply human tendency for selfishness to become sin expressed through indifference, exploitation and ignorance. Most consumers are in danger of being increasingly overwhelmed by a globalised market based on artificially encouraged and inflated desire – images and ideas of freedom reduced to fantasies of self – without any discipline of reflection or restraint. In fact real freedom is presented as stepping beyond these traditional frames. This is illustrated by the increasing emphasis upon children for labour and sexual exploitation. Maturity is seen as free expression with only the self as adjudicator. The result is a globalisation of indifference about how or by whom 'goods' (?!) are provided – or their fate after the event of consumption.

In this market environment there arises a need for satisfaction. The market pushes boundaries, especially into fantasy, minimising elements such as wider responsibilities or repercussions. The concentration is upon carefully chosen and constructed events to raise and satisfy desire. French theorists call this 'the libidinal economy'. Further, Helene Cixous emphasises the gendered nature of this world – seeing masculine desire as being for appropriation – 'to make the other one's own' – to possess, receive and again return. For Cixous the feminine allows the possibility of giving without expectation of return: true generosity. She uses the example of the maternal gift to the child, a full plenitude of giving into relationship which is material, and yet has less measurable outcomes or predictable satisfactions – and not primarily for the self but for the other.[2] In similar vein, Lucy Irigary interprets twenty-first century demand as a masculine form of demand based upon private property, expressed increasingly through a desire that particularly objectifies women – as is evident in fashion and in pornography.[3]

From Contract to Covenant

The challenge according to Bordieu is how to move from this egoistic, calculatory expression of desire, towards a more genuine reciprocity. One of the problems is the privatisation of personal identity. There is less emphasis or opportunity to express concern, kindness, or advice through face-to-face acts of charity. Yet these things create reciprocal relationships – mutuality, rather than fantasy disconnected from real lives. There is an urgent challenge to recognise real need and means of appropriate satisfaction on mutual terms.

Thus desire can be recognised as no longer for domination but for mutual flourishing. The Christian Gospel recognises that this assessment of desire and its social refinement is rooted in a certain understanding of what can be termed spirituality. Desire can be an expression of Spirit in and through the body, including in and through the body of society. Such a common Spirit illuminates a way to recognise a common Head and a common agenda (the kingdom). This is the focus of St Paul's letter to the Corinthians and his teaching about the Household. The key is to enable the surfacing and ownership of a 'spirit of unity', a sense of a common good. This is pursued and realised through personal service within the out flowing of the Master's generosity, through local performance in specific places, and within larger structures and systems.

This is the world of covenant rather than contract. An approach to relationship which can absorb the unevenness yet offer a common spirit of commitment, value and mutuality – a longer term journeying together for mutual well-being.

In the workings of the Christian tradition, T.T. Carter placed desire within the refining and healing frame of repentance, confession and absolution – the one thing missing in the twenty-first century marketing economy – which rather tries to develop established habits, eschewing any critical review.[4] The result is a continuing invitation to uncritical reinforcement and unfettered development. Any check or control is isolated and owned through the needs of each privatised individual self, or because of a lack of funds for purchase.

This is the world Hobbes recognised in his understanding of a social contract depending upon individual consent. The problem of this apparent commitment to a common basis of value is illustrated by the current explosion of Safeguarding legislation and attempted control which so often feels like a superficial endeavour that is not achieving much traction, because of the prevailing culture of individual desire seeking events of private satisfaction. The power and the rights of the purchaser rules supreme (the official ideology of the market). This masks the deep tendency of the shaping and suggestiveness of a market which learns our desires (Google or Facebook) and then enables commercial forces to manipulate them, all the time proclaiming a commitment to defend privacy!

The Christian calling of forming community provides a very contrary agenda. One based not on individuality but upon the incorporation of desire as a force to enable satisfaction with the other in a mutual flourishing and a common ownership of the realities of sin or falling short, and the consequent need for confession and absolution – to enable the well-being of the whole, and appropriate recovery from the human tendency and temptation towards self-centredness.

This presents a stark contrast to an approach which sees satisfaction as simply for the self, through others. By contrast, fulfilment through mutual giving requires a very different understanding of 'events' – as elements of the common life, so that exchange enables every participant to become a member of everyone else. For example, marriage is recognised as a social good in the community in the Christian understanding – not simply social or sexual desire as part of an essentially private partnership.

Underlying these issues about desire is the question of attitudes to power. Christians proclaim that Jesus is Lord – we are slaves, in one Household serving one Master: the mutual well-being which St Paul calls 'koinonia'. The market economy treats power as a personal possession, responsibility and opportunity – and thus works through competition not cooperation. In the language of Thomas Hobbes the key is what kind of sovereign power? One possibility is a contract overseen by the state or the market. The alternative is a more personal recognition of the Lordship of the Messiah and His all-inclusive agenda.

Christians have always recognised the value of proper organisation, whether through the Empire, nations or other political forms. Yet Jesus was clear that there would always be a distinction between the call to "Render to Caesar the things that are Caesar's, and to God the things that are God's" (Matthew 22:21). Similarly St Paul called upon disciples to obey the authorities since they have a vocation under God. Yet these important practical, organisational arrangements are always to be inhabited in the Spirit of covenant – a mutuality which puts the other first and claims no prior rights for the self.

Public Reflection

If desire is untrammelled it becomes a force for inequality and domination: this is the route of exploitation, as we see with forced labour, sexual exploitation, organ donation, forced marriage, forced begging, domestic servitude and forced drug distribution. Contemporary society tends to mask this inequality because the market glorifies difference, which subtly reinforces the autonomy of self or small groups (the echo chamber effect) and blinds to wider connectivity or mutuality that exists beneath any kind of desire.

Therefore Christian discipleship should encourage wider public reflection and debate about desire and about pleasure – which is a keyword emphasised by the market because it quickly calls attention to personal experience and judgement. However the market's highly organised, profitable and sometimes illegal operating promotes desire as pleasuring the self. Hence the importance of alternative models of genuine mutuality – whether the role of the Trinity as a community of mutuality, or the role of institutions, particularly the ecclesia as Household in local assemblies or manifestations. Individuals connect best to local community witness within the shaping role of law and policy frames. But the sheer complexity and hiddenness of market drivers requires more intentional public scrutiny.

The Schooling of Desire

According to Mauss the underlying issue is "the nature of the dream". Desire is an inner call, often responding to outer/external forces which assume a role in shaping how to handle it appropriately. In the nineteenth century the famous Brighton preacher F. W. Robertson argued that the decay in morals tended to precede the decay in institutions. Organisations can only flourish through an inner Spirit that provides connection and enables community. Thus desire must be 'schooled'.

More recently, Rowan Williams has stated that "only in the social exchange of kenotic selves, each giving beyond itself toward another, is God's image restored"[5]. Thus, for the Christian disciple desire is not about satisfaction of self, but faith to defer satisfaction while others struggle. To put the call and agenda of the Master first, at cost to self. Prayer is the means of becoming schooled in this essential and life-giving renunciation – a handing over of the self and of the community into the purposes and priorities of God, through self-critical reflection opening up an awareness of prophetic possibilities for the whole kingdom project.

Further, the disintegration of law and the untrammelled triumph of desire leads not only to selfishness, but increasingly towards hatred. Indifference to others becomes irritation at difference, or competition for more personally tailored satisfactions.

Freedom becomes entrepreneurial, based upon the capacity to adapt rather than to contribute to the whole. Morality gives way to the economic as the measure of desire and its fulfilment. The key is human calculation rather than divine blessing. The driver is that of cause and effect, pursued by passion for self-satisfaction. The political dissolves into populist appeals to moments of personal commitment. Accumulations of support for immediate goals, often at cost to those not noticed and generally hidden from the surface workings of society, because the aim is simply the satisfactions of its key members i.e. those with economic resources to order demand and desire.

The Celebration of Desire

Yet desire must not be seen as a negative or necessarily dangerous force – which can be the implication of some readings of St Paul's teaching. On 8 June 1941 in the University Church in Oxford C.S. Lewis preached a sermon at Evensong called "The Weight of Glory". In it he reflected on the nature of desire and the understandable tendency of religion to warn against the excesses of earthly desire, calling for more disciplined and controlled lives. Lewis recognised the danger of a puritanical idolatry of self-achievement through the apparently triumphant disciplining of desire. In a purple passage he encouraged people to be bolder in desire:

> "Our Lord finds our desires, not too strong, but too weak. We are half-hearted creatures, fooling about with drink and sex and ambition when infinite joy is offered to us, like an ignorant child who wants to go on making mud pies in a slum because he cannot imagine what is meant by the offer of a holiday at the sea. We are far too easily pleased".[6]

There is a nobility of desire – for God, for goodness, beauty and truth that shapes and controls all other desire. Augustine recognised this important refinement in the Christian understanding and handling of desire and the demands it subsequently makes, in his important distinction between caritas and cupidity. Caritas is the love of the supreme good, beauty, and truth, for its own sake: love God is the first and controlling commandment. Cupiditas is love for the self, measured in temporal rather than eternal terms.

Augustine writes: "I call 'charity' the motion of the soul towards the enjoyment of God for His own sake, and the enjoyment of one's self and one's neighbour for the sake of God: but 'cupidity' is a motion of the soul towards the enjoyment of oneself, one's neighbour or any corporeal thing for the sake of something other than God".[7]

Love is the energy that issues in desire. It needs to be properly ordered into a form of striving for the kingdom, and the humble place of the self within it. Worship, especially confession and absolution, provides a key ordering, using the resources of Scripture, divinely ordered ministry, and a joining together in prayer and praise which unites all participants in a desire to give thanks for grace and glory, to own our complicity in oppressing and excluding others and to accept the divine invitation to make a different contribution – that of a slave to the Masters vineyard.

In his Confessions, Augustine makes the important distinction between vice, which combines inordinate desire with arbitrary freedom, with virtue as desire ordered by a charity committed to receiving and sharing God's love.

The Cambridge Platonist Henry More makes a similar distinction when he talks about 'the negation of I-hood, and the accommodation of the human will to the divine'[8]:

> "That we should thoroughly put off, and extinguish our own proper will, and that being thus dead to ourselves, we may live also unto God, and do all things whatsoever by His Instinct, or plenary Permission".

The result of such spiritual formation enables an exuberant and positive outflow of desire, from "the inward flowing Wellspring of Life eternal", which raises the spirit and infuses with the blessing of fulfilling our particular calling within the unfolding of our mysterious creation.

The disappearance of the language of vice and virtue is an important indication of the challenge to recover Christian tools for combating the selfish limiting of desire to more immediate personal satisfactions, and to nourish a proper celebration and cultivation of the much richer and greater desire for God's promises being fulfilled – the invitation C.S. Lewis highlighted.

A challenge increasingly urgent in a market-driven ecology which is shaping Christian discipleship into a personal journey and private charitable responses – totally inadequate to halt the growth of systems and structures controlling demand and commodifying people so as to make profits from providing affordable satisfaction to personal desire through the hidden exploitation of others who are more vulnerable.

The nature of desire requires not just schooling and shaping, but critical judgement and firm boundaries. The gospel word is 'sin'. The softening pastoral effects of liberation have served to banish the word sin from public discourse, with the implication that judgement is privatised. Public authority provides rules and boundaries for driving on the roads, with proper policing and prohibiting penalties for transgression. But personal behaviour is much less clearly controlled. Hence the space for criminality and the enslaving exploitation of the vulnerable, especially children.

There is an urgent need for Christian disciples to own the sinful temptations towards self-satisfaction which form and drive a great deal of desire, both personal and institutional. Thus the importance of confession, absolution, forgiveness, and the owning of the vital roles of discipline, resisting very self-centred desires, and recognising grace as a healing gift without which evil tends to gain the upper hand. Then desire becomes destructive of true self, and of others.

Desire needs schooling and publicly agreed boundaries and controls. A massively countercultural message.

Endnotes

[1] M. Mauss. *The Gift: The Form and Reason for Exchange in Archaic Societies.* Routledge 1990.

[2] Helene Cixous. *The Newly Born Woman.* University of Minnesota Press 1980.

[3] Elizabeth Grosz. *Sexual Subversions.* Allen & Unwin 1989.

[4] Alastair Redfern. *The Clewer Initiative*. ISPCK 2017, p77.

[5] B. Myers. *Christ the Stranger: The Theology of Rowan Williams*. T & T Clark 2012.

[6] C.S. Lewis. *The Weight of Glory and other Addresses*. Eerdmans 1965.

[7] Augustine. *On Christian Doctrine*. Translated by D. W. Robertson, 1858 3.10.16.

[8] A. Lichtenstein. *Henry More*. Harvard UP 1962, p6.

Questions For Further Reflection And Group Discussion

1. How do you think your demand as a consumer is stimulated and satisfied?

2. What is the role of repentance, confession and absolution in our handling of desire?

3. Can prayer be an effective means for "schooling" desire? Think of some examples.

4. How do you understand the difference between cupidity and charity?

CHAPTER - 4

Morality

Three Moralities

Michael Oakeshott in his book 'Morality and Politics' argues that in the last five hundred years there have been three contrasting moralities or 'moral dispositions'[1]. First, he identifies 'the morality of community ties'. This is a community not of association or choice, but of family and place. The self is known through being a member and through the recognition of rules, overseers and mutualities.

Second, Oakeshott describe a 'morality of individuality': defined as 'the disposition to make choices for oneself to the maximum possible effect'. In other words morality is shaped to seek conditions in which the fruit of these choices can best be enjoyed, often helped by technology. The key is individual conscience and privacy – he refers to Descartes "Cogito ergo sum". The outcome creates associations, not communities – and religious festivals are replaced by bank holidays i.e. finance is owned as the primary common denominator. The triumph of mammon in terms of chapter two.

Third he outlines "the morality of the displaced", i.e. those not able (because of circumstance or ability or other factors) to pursue their choices or follow the shaping forces of the market. The vulnerable and the poor become people of frustrated desire and their frame for relationships becomes essentially negative – dependent upon the unlikely and uncontrollable promises of others. A culture of those who are desperate to respond to any invitation. In this sense the exploited are the victim of the other two moralities of choice, and also complicit in pursuing and participating in the values and practices of the market – by chasing the promises and conforming to desire as self-satisfaction. As community and individual flourishing both dissolve, many are left 'lacking confidence or capacity' to manage, either on their own, or within their needy peer group.

Popular media tends to disguise this displacement by focusing on examples as exceptions, or by hiding them from fashionable views. There are few attempts to recognise these needy people as signs or sacraments of society's problems in the manner of E.B Pusey who argued for priority being given to the response to the poor because of their privileged role, in helping to identify and proclaim the Good News.[2] Such displaced elements in a society become fodder for mass movements – as is evident in Trumpism, Right wing extremism, or other forms of misleading promises which will in fact lead to exploitation.

Increasing Vulnerability

From the nineteenth century there was a tendency to look to government to order morality and its outworkings, hence the development of the welfare state. As the state is now withdrawing from such corporate responsibilities, the temptation to keep this displaced element hidden increases, as does the use of liberal laws which magnify the value of 'difference', including a vast disparity of lifestyle and opportunities. The result is to simply disguise the issue or give society permission to categorise needs as an inevitable ingredient of pluralism. In fact the displaced are increasingly excluded from the culture of enterprise – which therefore creates a distinct form of experience and expression of exploitation from which Modern Slavery recruits. The liberal smokescreen for this process of exclusion and annihilation is the increasingly loud rhetoric about human rights.

This collapse of communal order and the ensuing reign of the individual leaves millions lost, unprotected, leaderless and homeless in terms of security and of place. Here lies the root of the contemporary rise in vulnerability, denied any sense of belonging and allowed very restricted access to education and material resources.

The media construction of new forms of common good as echo chambers which tantalise and advertise individual desire and its personal (selfish) satisfactions, serves to further emphasise exclusion, especially because slogans and tweets give the impression of hope – whereas in fact such hope is disconnected from the reflection and wider community contextualisation which Households and localised awareness provide in order to discern failings and frustrations, and thus identify appropriate counter responses. A process illustrated in parables, miracles and the general style of New Testament teaching which presupposes an overall connecting context of Kingdom or Body to hold together disparate parts in a common flourishing.

A narrowly individual focus turns Christian justice into charity through the prioritisation of individual choice. A positive act of self-affirming experience. By contrast the Messiah bears scars of defeat, the marks of complexity and challenge in human systems. For Christians following this slave -like way of sacrificial service, the poor, the vulnerable and the victims become the sites and signs of challenge and of opportunity for defining and realising the content and the outcomes of Christian morality. Most especially those people who are traded as commodities within the market system, becoming the spoil of consumers seeking the satisfaction of tailored, personalised desires. A graphic example would be the marketing of vulnerable children on the dark web for sexual exploitation – a practice void of almost any moral frame or discipline. Christian morality recognises the importance of acknowledging our debt to the vulnerable – as revealers and markers of what new life might look like and how it could be known, tasted, shared and pursued – by mutual partnership and the exploration of new models.

One Body

The determining sign is that of the inclusivity and practical materiality of the Eucharist: " This is my Body ", creates a physical and social construct which included slaves as full members, as in Paul's Households of faith. Here is the seed of a new corporation, a model for business, for families, for gatherings and groupings. The role of the Clewer Initiative is to cross cultural, social and economic boundaries in order to create new forms of connection, expressed in new approaches to business, opening up an alternative participatory politics, and better-connected groupings of faith and community organisations: a good example would be the Hidden Voices project. Such endeavours will better join together debtors (most of us) and creditors (the vulnerable/slaves) in receiving universal credit that is the unconditional love of God.

In this way all are invited to acknowledge being indebted to the One/Father, and all are called to slavery in the Household, which in New Testament times could include the enslaved in trusted and essential roles. In the latter part of the twentieth century, through liberation theology, the poor were the key to understanding the Gospel and the call of the kingdom. More recently those who are enslaved are assuming this key indicative role, not least because 'enslaved' is a radically inclusive term for Christian thinking and practice - inviting and mixing those formally enslaved to others, and those of us enslaved to self, not therefore through a binary judgementalism, but by means of a complex of interdependence and mutual responsibilities. The danger for faith-based contributors is an expectation that the enslaved will conform to 'our' values and frames of reference, our limited morality. Christian morality is unitary, inclusive, based upon universal credit – all are sinners, all are invited to be saved (or made healthy in God). This is highlighted in the story of the blind man in John 9, and his refrain "I was blind, now I can see". Here is the testimony of the vulnerable, the man enslaved to physical blindness. Yet the call and invitation to healing is equally to experts in vision and right performance – the Pharisees and the authorities - as much as those so blatantly excluded and unnoticed.

The Eucharistic fellowship which creates the new corporation presupposes the fraction of embodiments – ours, others, societies – through a common experience of the forgiveness of sins and the unmerited gift of absolution. This recognises the reality of a co-mingling narrative of surface roles – slaves, masters, change agents, and a uniting spiritual call to kenosis, seeking the lowest place for the sake of others, especially those in most need. This is not an easy calling to discern or to follow.

The Management of Morality
Foucault, in 'The Birth of Biopolitics' remarks that Homo oeconomicus "appears precisely as someone manageable.....

someone who is eminently governable". This kind of encultured dependency drives the market and the hierarchy of control and exploitation, so that "desire is conformed to commodifiable options".[3]

The market therefore shapes power as the basis of a morality that claims to be neutral, realistic and historically inevitable, even positively beneficial – not least because the market presents an apparently limitless choice and thus potential for huge confusion and pressure, without any overall guidance or shaping of these market forces. Such outcomes are evident in advertising and the arena of fashion, which aim to capture and direct the 'self' while perpetuating an illusion of being free and in control because of the constant mantra of choice being the key measure of desire and satisfaction.

The moral challenge for the Gospel is how to encourage and enable interconnectivity not through the markets pressurising the choices of desiring individuals, but through the values of the heart, expressed in the Beatitudes and through the neighbour as incontrovertibly part of our 'Household' or lived-in space. Thus the moral aim should be to work together to discover and deploy the tools and trajectories that bind and heal (religare). In this way immorality is identified, so that instead of every self becoming an island amidst a sea of technologically driven possibilities in a manner divorced from social responsibilities and assessed through the narrowingly artificial categories of gender, sexuality and individuality – all attuned to being appropriated by separate choice made by each self – rather there can instead be a shift from instant gratification to awareness of an eternal present, which is being aware of living in the presence of Christ.

This kind of identity requires not a DIY self-constructed shelter and pleasure ground, but the losing of self (kenosis) in the sacred, transcendent aspiration of the human heart in all its fullness. Such morality is best explored and expressed through prayer as a more self-conscious discipline to reflect on the universality of failure and missing the mark or sin, and instead to seek guidance and inspiration to learn to privilege the other, particularly the vulnerable – in the way of Christ. In this sense there is a key role within the Christian understanding of morality for what might be termed 'dissolution'. Not dissolution as the terror of modernity dissolving and increasing an anxiety for self-survival, but rather dissolution of self into the new corporation of the Christ.

Morality and Mysticism

This will be increasingly important as the state retreats and gives up any pretence of spiritual ordering or oversight – a phenomenon which in the nineteenth and twentieth centuries was termed being public spirited. This highlights the importance of mysticism for morality. An ordered reflection beyond the known, into the cloud of unknowing. A wider step into deeper reality, only perceived by human tools as through a glass darkly. Such a spirituality includes suffering being explored not just as a problem to be solved, but also as a place of revelation. A classic example would be the witness and teachings of St John of the Cross. Here lies a different source of power, accessed through humility, confession, the gift of forgiveness and a new ability to recognise the important contribution of the hidden voices of victims.

Further, morality is essentially expressed in action, which always creates rather than closes down, and offers signs of character and value (Blondel). Using action as the locus of revelation enables knowing and being known to arise through the social processes of life, through the unfolding of corporations in all their various forms. In this way action becomes an enabler of self-transcendence, entering into the context of others and of the Other. Thus action points towards the journey and towards the process of the mystic – whereby morality is weighed, angled and applied, but always in a deeply reflective context, open to the mystery of new insights, especially from darkness and dark places, thus enabling the essential and mysterious dynamic between promise and performance, hope and so called reality.

Henry Scott Holland recognised that experience is reality known not just by impression, but by the coming together of ourselves with something else – involving an inward and outward element. In this dynamic, moral sensing and focus is never simply subjective, but always engages with what to each of us is 'given'. Our examination of such an encounter opens experience to critique, and a different kind of affirmation. In this way morality operates within a certain instability and unknowness, hence the importance of the mystical, of reflection, of trust in promise and the possibility of richer revelation as guidance that connects with the heart long before our rational faculties can try to turn such insights into some form of knowledge.

Service not Structures

This kind of morality includes a servant element, not simply structures. The approach will involve the gathering of a variety of challenges and complexities around power, exploitation, story, capacity to notice the unnoticed, and challenge us to be honest about exclusion and invisibility. In this way morality can unfold seeking guidance together with others within such a mix. Most importantly, the inclusion of the contribution of those who are speechless, because of their experience, trauma and struggles for self-expression, highlight how much can be learned, especially to inform those who indirectly patronise exploitation through being consumers or investors. 1 Corinthians 12:25 "if one member suffers, all suffer together". Thus our identity within a moral system is never what we think it is, because of our limited ability to see, experience and articulate, and because of other essential actors who are not easily noticed, alongside the challenge to discern and acknowledge the hidden powers of structures and systems. In this way morality ceases to be about demonising and romanticising, both of which tend to take shortcuts by monopolising ideas and action plans. Instead there needs to be a deeper ontological level of encounter and engagement which always enriches participants from every conceivable perspective. This process will unfold through the interplay of promise, confession and forgiveness i.e. a sacramental joining together in the Masters generosity to inform a properly viable morality, one which can be more fully developed 'in Christ', despite our failings and complicities.

Thus morality is no longer confined to the arena of quantitative measurement, particularly round the notion of individual satisfaction, as the sole means of recognising and assessing reality. Instead values such as common goodness and the beauty that touches the humanness of hearts, become not the minority interest of religion or old-fashioned politics, but rather the stuff of common reflection, ownership of failings, and aspiration for new life together in a radical complementarity which overcomes the separations of selfishness, and enables mutuality of interchange driven by slave -like service of the needs of the other. A spirit to inform structures, not to be conformed to them.

Endnotes

[1] M. Oakeshott. *Morality and Politics in Modern Europe.* Yale 1993.

[2] E. B. Purey. *Parochial Sermons.* Harvard 1958. Oxford 1865.

[3] M. Foucault. *The Birth of Biopolitics.* Palgrave 1979 (2008), p270.

Questions For Further Reflection And Group Discussion

1. What does the reality of poverty and exclusion reveal about the workings of contemporary society?

2. Do slavery to others and slavery to self have common features? Identify three examples.

3. Living in the presence of Christ is to be aware of an eternal present, and not to be driven by the forces of instant gratification. How do we discern the differences and act accordingly.

4. How can morality be grounded in the Master's generosity, so as to produce a public spirituality of values and practices?

PART THREE
Power and Powerlessness

CHAPTER - 5

Victims and Justice

Victim Identity

The language and categorisation of victims is often more readily adopted by would-be helpers, than those who are actually suffering from poverty or oppression. In an empirical study entitled "Relative Deprivation and Social Justice: A Study of Attitudes to Social Inequality in Twentieth-Century England". W.G. Runciman concluded that "many people at the bottom of society are less resentful of the system, and many nearer to the top are also, than their actual position appears to warrant".[1]

This would reflect a major issue in the fight against Modern Slavery. Sometimes those enslaved are reluctant to accept rescue or freedom, partly because the conditions from which they came in order to become trapped in Modern Slavery could seem even more brutal and limiting; and partly because of the skilled recruitment techniques of criminal gangs, which stem from a business model that identifies people who can be easily dominated and made massively dependent: those who are homeless, suffering from broken relationships, or with mental health issues, for example.

From the other perspective, that of would-be rescuers and helpers, there is rarely a consistent understanding of the framework of justice within which rescue, or restorative, and preventative work is unfolding. Much effort is localised, personalised, and pragmatic in terms of what might seem to be feasible regarding the policies and practices of local partners such as the police or other statutory agencies. Thus 'victims' becomes a term that all can recognise to describe the enslaved, thereby limiting the potential contribution of how people might shift from such a position, and toward what kind of goals. 'Victim' becomes a negative term to control and limit assessment of particular situations, and not a helpful term to indicate priorities and practices that could be truly transformative, opening up possibilities rather than closing all into a negative designation.

Of course justice must be essentially experiential for all concerned, yet any articulation of this oppression needs to become quickly connected with paths of transformative new possibilities – both in terms of practical living arrangements such as housing, jobs and security, and also in terms of aspiration for progress, recovery and new nourishment.

Hence justice for victims needs to be linked to work about public policy, legal and social frameworks, and the provision of more secure, sustainable employment and living opportunities. For the church this witness and way was clearly articulated by Lesslie Newbigin:

> "in its liturgy it continually relives the mystery of God's action in justifying the ungodly. In its corporate life and the mutual care and discipline of its members it embodies (even if very imperfectly), the justice of God which both unmasks the sin and restores relations with the sinner. In its action in the society of which it is part it will seek to be with Jesus among those who are pushed to the margins. But in all this it will point beyond itself and its own weakness and

ambivalence, to the One in whom God's justice has been made manifest by the strange victory of the cross.....It can continually nourish a combination of realism and hope which finds expression in concrete actions which can be taken by the local community and more widely, which reflect and embody the justice of God".[2]

Forgiveness and Grace

The theological priority properly afforded to the victim is rooted in the key foundation to human flourishing – the ability to forgive. The only phrase in the Lord's prayer demanding anything of human being is "as we forgive those who sin against us". The challenge of Jesus to Peter's question about the scope of forgiveness is not once, or even seven times, but seventy times seven times (Luke 17:4) indicates the scale of the challenge, and of the possible outcomes. Forgiveness flows from the innocent victim (slave) on the cross – because "they know not what they do". Individuals, groups, nations, religions, all contribute to the making of injustice. It is the innocent victim who needs to begin the possibility of healing and new ways. A process which unfolds without knowing the outcomes – a prophetic path of faith which can flow from the victim, through their supporters, to be light and leaven into the wider world.

But forgiveness is always attended by the possibility of failure, and thus risks engagement with political realities. W.H. Auden pointed out that such forgiveness is always an action, not a reaction.[3] This kind of healing action is a positive strategy that interrupts the normal course of balancing cause and effect, and just desserts, and introduces a new way of radical mutuality – faith to enter together into a common Household.

In this sense victims need to be identified and supported in such a Household endeavour, as do would-be helpers and supporters – statutory and voluntary. New life emerges between people of different experiences and perspectives, not simply through the necessary and important working out of strategies based upon reason, assessment and joint planning: but also through a common spirit of a forgiving generosity that can enable deeper bonds and a more adventurous stepping into the future together. Grace needs to surround and mediate the importance of law.

The result is that working with victims becomes a route for the construction of a kind of social capital that can transform rescue, preventative and supportive endeavours into part of a broader movement to release new energies and models for social justice. For the kind of human flourishing which best reflects the coming of the kingdom for which Christians pray daily. The result is a public spirituality which can create wider connectivities and inspire greater aspirations of human hearts to be joined in a mutual flourishing which brings much greater degrees of hope and quality of living together.

Representatives

Nonetheless, many who are victims, will not be willing or ready to contribute directly to such an ecology. The effects of oppression and abuse, together with the widespread recruitment into modern slavery of people who are particularly fragile and vulnerable, means that many victims require space, and a gentle, permissive approach to healing. This fact emphasises the importance of representation.

Amidst the interplay between victims and agencies of support, rescue and prevention, there is a special role for those who can help the victim to be heard, through careful listening, sensitive re-articulation and translation, and an ability to broker and bridge these insights, experiences and aspirations into the broader areas of public policy, improved practices, and the development of new models of 'Household'. The calling out and overseeing of the new bonds of association and mutuality helps to fulfil the victim offering of forgiveness and new life and generate a more inclusive connectivity that religious people call catholic.

Too often the various networks and agencies involved in working with victims develop a protective identity and trajectory that soon has the effect of translating victim experience and aspiration into already defined channels of interpretation and progression. Not the strategy of an ever including 'Household', but rather the performance -related approach of a corporation wanting to be successful according to measurable and demonstrable criteria. This is an especially dangerous temptation to statutory and voluntary bodies needing to justify budget allocations and funding.

Further, representation can free many of these key actors, as well as victims themselves, from becoming diverted into wider agendas than their particular remit. There is a priestly, mediatorial role which people of faith, and especially their recognised leaders, can offer. A role not based upon particular expertise around all the complex issues involved, but rather based upon a call to join all these endeavours and perspectives in a common spirit of generous forgiveness and mutual commitment, to cooperate for the wider purposes of bringing forth the kind of new living which heralds the transformation of societies.

Power as Pluriform

Such a 'Spirit' searches not for narrow conformity, but rather for a generous and trusting contribution to outcomes too great for any particular agency to fully understand or deliver. There needs to be a strong element of reflective learning together, with the voices of victims represented as central, and a key testing frame for values and ways of implementing progress.

The formal authorities will need narrower and more clearly defined processes but must be challenged to place this essential contribution within the framework of a public spirituality that allows them to acknowledge the importance of the victim voice, and their own limitations in listening and interpreting. Power then becomes pluriform and produced through such mutuality. An ingredient in the self-sacrificing mix which enables justice to emerge as new life for all the participants, not just for the victims. The latter are not a crude measure for perfect solutions, but leaven and light for the journey to enable recovery from sinful oppression and openness to new light and hope.

Victims can thus enable the debt owed to them by an uncaring and unnoticing society, to become a forgiving of debts accompanied by the important work of identifying new and better ways for all. These debts as forgiven can create a new kind of credit – modelled by the creative generosity of victims and capable of becoming the seed of the means of creating new possibilities. The victims become key investors in an investment partnership. No longer the binary judgementalism that perpetuates categorisations into victim or perpetrator, sinned against or sinner. Rather the creation of new including networks of generosity and mutuality. This is the proper project of liberation, opening up entry into a complex body, with many parts joined in a common spirit that can lead, inspire and enable. Power gathered and expressed through pluriformity.

Projects as Models

The key is the development of real projects in real time, which begin to demonstrate the viability and the power of networks created in this spirit of mutuality and the unfolding of specific arenas of the new life. These projects will help improve or modify existing structures and priorities. An important contribution in a time when expectations of government roles in combating modern slavery and creating viable economic and social environments are becoming lower, due to issues of resourcing and political coherence.

The growth of the new tribalisms, from Facebook pages to populist causes, needs the counterforce of a richer, more inclusive model of networking, around the learning that can be made available from those at the sharp end of these tribal failures – the excluded and the unnoticed.

This deeper truth about the potential for human being needs to be made manifest. Attempts to explain and capture an understanding of it will always be subsequent and secondary. The desperate plight of victims demands this ordering of priorities, and provides the resources for appropriate responses, which will be always partial, but progressive in real contexts and everyday lives. The aim is incremental progress that has effect across a wide range of those involved, rather than sharp solutions for the most apparently powerless. The faith to form partnerships which can embark on projects – while wider strategies will remain subject to continuing adjustment.

These new models will include learning from victims that dispossession and marginalisation can be important perspectives from which to evaluate current systems and values. Their voices can interrupt current complacencies and evoke the courage to join together in new approaches. Such action unites and enables a connectivity which can be continually strengthened through sharing across incompletenesses. Thus institutional arrangements will be always subject to review and restructuring, the key driver being the gracious inclusivity which ever emanates from the forgiving spirit offered through the experiences of innocent victims.

Instability Needs Mercy

Thus there needs to be a doctrine of institutional instability, reflecting the experience of instability central to victimhood, and owning this dispossession as giving the possibility of new and richer life, through a generous connectivity with all kinds of other actors. The measure will not be the coherence of beliefs or strategies, but the effectiveness of engagement – the resurrection of the dead i.e. victims and all who are engaged in enabling, allowing or ignoring victimisation. The focus is not, therefore, what participants have in common, but in an emerging vision informed by the dispossession of the victim and empowered by a public spirituality of sympathetic respondents and joint work to craft better possibilities for all. A method Blondel termed "co-action": or in the words of the nineteenth century pioneer against sex trafficking, T.T. Carter "compassion, the sharing of mercy" as a gift we are each capable of receiving and offering.

The result is a stability rooted in a common journey, informed from any incidents and experiences of failure and suffering, rather than the buttresses which create the immobility of traditional organisational stability. Power is perceived and handled differently, because of the conscious appeal to the priority of victim contributions, generally mediated through representative ministries. The heart holds the keys and frames the work of the head. This is the proper basis for productive participation: the life of the inclusive Household wherein the measure for continuing life together is especially shaped by those who seem to benefit least – often by having been excluded and unnoticed.

A Continuing Passion Story

In Christian terms the presence of the victim provides a witness and an invitation to acknowledge the prolonged passion narrative within which human life continues to unfold. The sign of the Slave and the Lamb amidst the unruly forces of human lust and domination. This dynamic continues and is constitutive of the unfolding of creation. Hence today, as in Jerusalem on the occasion of the crucifixion, the forces of political and religious systematisation devise hierarchies of control aimed at containing suffering, so that victims need to conform to established norms or pay the price. The established norms of personalised desire and private morality increasingly trap millions in subjection and exploitation. There is a refusal to recognise the wisdom of the Psalmist that "night to night declares knowledge" (Psalm 19). In the continuing Passion narrative light comes from darkness, life from death, truth from the underside of human systems and confidence.

The Gospel is not to be adapted to fit contemporary conditions, including so much unnoticed oppression. Rather it explores the unfolding narrative of a slave people, the followers of a slave, so that the stories of those immersed in this experience of restriction, dependency and the cry for release, can illuminate and inspire the wider story and it's more inclusive development. The Good News operates not through narrowing dogma, but through "memories subversive of unfreedom".[4]

Such voices always enable the interpreter to stand outside of the common assumptions of their times, and to pursue deeper, more mysterious manifestations of the 'way', thereby generating new agendas and illumination. In this way the memory and the voice of the victims provides vital resources not just for rescue, or for rehabilitation, but for new life: "a new reconciliation which includes and celebrates what has been hidden and oppressed and exploited".[5]

Thus the experience and memory of unfreedom (slavery) becomes the seed of imagination, hope and new possibilities (salvation).

Night to Night Declares Knowledge

A practical manifestation of the prophetic effects of such practice would be the experience of Josephine Butler, the nineteenth century campaigner on behalf of prostitutes and their presumed guilt. Their stories highlighted the reality of what was called a 'double standard' . Women and men expected to observe high standards of sexual morality, yet many women being drawn by the purchasing power of powerful men into a very different set of standards, for individuals, for the family, and for public behaviour. The result of this interpretation of the experience of the victims of such sex slavery was to recognise the gendered blindness of much nineteenth century morality and legislation, and to highlight the hypocrisy of a public narrative so contrary to the evidence of those subjected to exploitation and exclusion.

The experience of the victim is no longer to be forgotten, or 'healed' to allow uncritical conformity to contemporary values. Rather such experience can enable what has been hidden and ignored to become the source of new life – a resurrection from the tomb of execution: new life through a crucified slave. Night to night declares knowledge (Psalm 19:2).

Endnotes

[1] W. G. Runciman. *Relative Deprivation and Social Justice: A study of Attitudes to Social Inequality in Twentieth-Century England.* University Of California Press, 1966, p3.

[2] Lesslie Newbigin. *Whose Justice.* The Economical Review Vol 44, 3. p308–311.

[3] M. L. Knott. *Unlearning with Arendt.* Other Press 2013, p12.

[4] M. L. Lamb. *Solidarity With Victims.* Crossroad 1982, p110.

[5] J. B. Metz and J. Moltmann. *Faith and the Future.* Concilium 1995, p17.

Questions For Further Reflection And Group Discussion

1. *In what ways can forgiveness create new possibilities, especially when the victim has hitherto been in forced silence, hidden in plain sight?*

2. *Can victims be represented in ways which offer empowerment and yet avoid creating unhelpful pressures?*

3. *What might be the role of religious leadership in this process?*

4. *Identify six contributions that the experience of victims can make towards improving current understandings and practices.*

CHAPTER - 6

Sovereignty and Lordship

Prayer

For many people the instinct to pray, to place oneself in the larger and more mysterious context of being a creature in a Creation brimming with power and purpose, becomes reduced to an anxious desire to seek/demand what seems best for 'my' immediate self. This secular kind of prayer seeks support and confidence for the personal journey and those valued or involved as part of it.

By contrast, the prayer of the creature to the Creator is an offering of self into a perspective of being able to see more deeply into the promises and possibilities that the heart is made to pursue relationship through a love which gives as well as takes. A consciousness of the image of God in every other creature, and a real sense of mutuality within the kingdom project.

In this sense the Lord God is owned as Sovereign or Master, not to simply hand over every concern, but rather to recognise that each person, being created in the image of the Creator, is a precious and responsible part of the unfolding of life and its proper fulfilment. Thus a tension arises, within each person, and in the relations of people with one another, between the seeking for self-satisfaction and the call to become part of a wider, universalising endeavour – the rule of God. This latter calling is accessed by accepting a real dependency upon the mysterious callings of the Master. An invitation to become a slave to His purposes, in ways that will often seem costly to the more obvious and immediate concerns that can be perceived by the individual, thinking only of themselves.

Poverty Provides The Agenda

This position of absolute dependency requires the response of faith and indicates the importance of the victim – the excluded and oppressed – in exposing and inhabiting the arenas in need of the healing of grace and goodness: the conjoining presence and power of Divine purpose inspiring human life.

What liberation theologians call 'the civilisation of wealth' indicates a world organised around the resourcing of 'selves', often to ridiculous degrees, as a prioritisation that condemns the great bulk of people to real poverty. Sovereignty is lodged in controllable measures for immediate personal benefit, rather than in audacious generosity to include others as the key purpose.

The Lord's statement that "you will always have the poor with you" clarifies the calling of disciples – to notice and respond to this ever-prevalent reality of a more limited and oppressive form of sovereignty being ever constructed by human endeavour. Thus the victims become the touchstone for being able to discern and respond to true sovereignty, as the parable of the sheep and the goats in Matthew 25 makes quite clear.

Yet much political, economic, social and religious life treats the victims as a problem to be managed, rather than as the key to the discernment of human callings and challenges. Sovereignty for human living is discerned in the One who chose to be recognised as a slave – a victim. Thus Ignacio Ellacuria calls for a "civilisation of poverty", not to make everyone poor, but in order to identify the key principles for human organisation and priorities.[1] To begin from the perspective of the victim which calls out a different kind of creativity and connectivity, including an acknowledgement of the importance of work, in an economic system too focused on capital as the engine of wealth creation.

The Gospel accounts highlight the sheer complexity of victimhood. The socially excluded - lepers and mentally ill. The religiously marginalised – prostitutes and tax collectors. The culturally oppressed – women and children. The socially dependent – widows and orphans. The physically handicapped – death, dumb, crippled and blind. The psychologically tormented – the possessed and epileptic. Such complexity provides an understandable barrier to the crafting of victim-based responses.

However there is a more basic and inclusive categorisation of being a victim: slavery – to self, to wealth, to human systems of security which protects some (the few) by excluding others (an increasing majority). Such slavery is nourished by the superficial approach of many contemporary values. This is why the concentration upon including the perspective and experience of those at the sharpest points of being victimised, the largely hidden and brutally abused sisters and brothers caught up in modern slavery, provides a particularly important opportunity to critique a civilisation of wealth, and to explore the cultivation of a civilisation of poverty, based upon the emergence of new, more including Households and networks.

Such an alternative sovereignty requires the voice of the victim to be more clearly identified and amplified, otherwise the reality of the human situation becomes obscured and unrecognised. Sobrino charges the Western Church with exchanging such a prophetic strategy for a partial and largely complicit engagement with the expanding complexities of a liberal ethics that presuppose individual autonomies and the right to provide for the self as a major preoccupation.

This temptation has increased with the collapse of inclusive liberalism and the fragility of the market focused upon wealth creation. The result is the tendency for those in power to create a perpetual state of emergency, stoking an anxiety which encourages even more focus upon the self and providing for its survival and security. Dependency becomes a source of fear and leads to projection upon populist moments of seeking solidarity. Such moments promise the mechanism to provide long-term security. They tend to focus like a post on the Facebook page, providing a sign of the sovereignty of the self-seeking solace in accumulating a respectable number of 'likes'.

The transcendence which gathers all these separated and anxious identities into a greater whole needs a different kind of investment, one which trusts in being a mere part, needing others to share in a bold project to live with vulnerability, yet saving each other from victimisation through practising a radical mutuality. All are invited to share in the sovereignty of the Master – the Lordship of the Christ or Messiah.

Management As The Highest Aim

Foucault recognised that the amazingly inclusive image of the one Shepherd and the one flock, to include some at present not even recognised as potential members, has been replaced by a different interpretation of the pastor. The therapeutic minister to the stresses of autonomous subjects on a personal faith journey has become the dominant model. This alternative pastoral strategy becomes a subtle support to the civilisation of wealth, assuming the fundamental call to be one of providing resources for the modern freedoms of individual survival. Thus ministry moves from the prophetic leadership of the Shepherd, who led the flock through the wilderness as sovereign, to the supportive pastoral care that follows the lead of each sheep, with as much personal nourishment as can be managed. In fact the task of such ministry becomes management for the small number that can be serviced, rather than leadership of entire, inclusive communities and their common aspirations.

Such a shift has encouraged faith groups to approach the phenomenon of the victim in this latter mode of seeking appropriate care for each individual. Thereby creating a management task of impossible proportions and offering support to statutory agencies that encourages them to conform uncritically to the civilisation of wealth which in fact is designed to create victims. There have always been 'slaves' servicing various systems of desire and demand within the civilisation of wealth.

Strategies within this ecology of the sovereignty of self tend to focus upon enterprise to provide ministry from a variety of perspectives. And as the modern media creates cognitive dissonance whereby people are constantly distracted and drawn in by stimuli and information, so stress and insecurity increases, and pastoral need claims an adherence to the Shepherd who follows the sovereignty of those who seek attention. This whole process makes it even easier for dark forces to hide and hurt victims ever more effectively.

In his sermon "The Religion of the Day" Newman recognised that amidst the growing liberalism and individualism of industrialised society the ethical requirements of the wholly including law of the 'Spirit of Life', were softened down into something less strict, less un- earthy, less far reaching. The world seem to say "we will take such part of Christianity suits us, or else we will not take it at all".[2] The church has largely organised around this viewpoint and called it mission.

Victimhood Points Towards Victory

The incarnation, from birth in a stable to death on the cross, provides an outward sign of victimhood, yet it is from this trajectory of sacrificial service of a greater cause, that the glory of the salvation of the world emerges. This inward dimension is the Spirit of Holiness that is better able to be discerned in a civilisation of poverty.

In this way the victim becomes the source of true sovereignty, a sacrament of the salvation which emerges from a common dependency, a common slavery illuminated by the way of the slave who was the Saviour. Yet, just as criminality is creating modern slavery, so the complicity of the market demand that asks few questions of the choices being made by autonomous, free individuals, and the supportive pastoral ministry of faith groups, combine to obscure this offer of salvation to all, and keep the focus upon slavery to the self and some of its abominable expressions of abuse and exploitation.

Thus there is an urgent challenge to the church not simply to support victimhood, or even raise debate about values and systems, but, more, to bring to the light the real-time workings of injustice, through identifying and giving voice to the victims whose experience and need exposes most clearly the responses which must be made. Looking and listening needs analysis and action to promote prophetic new models of inclusion and mutuality. Much of the teaching of Jesus, as of Paul, presupposes an initial response through the unlikely partnership of Master and slave, the seeding of new experiences and aspirations. A very different route to freedom (salvation) than that negotiated around abstract notions of human rights that can never be uniformly claimed or enforced.

The Gospel works through the sovereignty of witness, not through that of macro oversight which always ends up by supporting a civilisation of wealth, i.e. the sovereignty of the self-expressed through those selves most able to set up care and flourishing arrangements for themselves.

Confession And Crucifixion

Thus the need to recover a more public and social sense of confession, penance and acknowledgement of falling short of the sovereign demands of the Creator and sustainer of all life. There are signs of some kind of public, strategic 'confession' round the call of saving the planet, but few signs of such an important discipline and prophetic searching around the increasing victimisation of people.

When there is a shift from principles to testimony, then there arises real, substantial evidence for confession and the seeking of a radical mutuality based on forgiveness and new ways of living together in a single ecosystem – the body of humanity: the body of creation: the body of Christ. With such possibilities emerging there is a crucial need to counter an uncritical faith in the power of technology to solve problems and provide salvation, by moving towards reading the register through the power released by acknowledging human failings and owning our ability to be forgiven, renewed and connected in a greater, more wholesome, common cause.

The prophetic tradition arises not from the fact that different interest groups design and solidify in terms of systems of understanding and practice, but from owning the imperfection of all endeavours, and the continuing need of the healing grace of human community (koinonia), ministry most especially to the victims of previous failings. This is the way of the cross, always the path to redemption and resurrection.

True justice emerges not from a binary choice between good and evil. Rather it emerges from confronting failure and shortcomings, and together seeking to live more fully in a graceful mutuality. Reality is always complex and beyond an easy reduction to human analysis and the subsequent creation of facts. Life unfolds through living – the sovereign power of the Master issues in a Holy Spirit that gives life and restores life. Human schemes and systems are vital, but always in need of prophetic critique and revision, working through frailty and faith. Justice always emerges from injustice in a fallen world. Victims are the barometer: sovereignty is in the Spirit giving fullness of life.

The New Solidarity For Salvation

For Paul the collection for the poor became the one way of creating solidarity within and between the Households of Faith, and of making a credible witness to the wider world about this distinctive calling and contribution to the proper flourishing of Creation.

As he makes clear in Romans 15:2 "he who loves the other has fulfilled the law". There could be no more stark challenge to his stratified and separated society. Hence the vital image of the body in Romans 12 with so many different parts yet bound together in a single calling and expression of the wonder of creation.

Endnotes

[1] Ignacio Ellacuria and Jon Solosino. *Mysterium Liberations: Fundamental Concepts in Liberation Theology*. Orbis 2004.

[2] J. H. Newman. *Parochial Sermons* Vol.I Rivingtons 1875, p24.

Questions For Further Reflection And Group Discussion

1. *Can a civilisation of wealth learn to become a civilisation of poverty? What would be the key marks?*

2. *Should the Shepherd follow the flock and concentrate upon caring for stragglers, or lead the flock into new pastures of hope and collective well-being? Share your experiences.*

3. *What might the sovereignty of witness look like?*

4. *How might public confession and penance about saving the planet embrace the need to save human victims too? Write a liturgy that could be used in your local church.*

PART FOUR
Gospel Resources

CHAPTER - 7

The Slave who Serves the Master

A Master In Israel

"Now there was a Pharisee named Nicodemus, a leader of the Jews. He came to Jesus by night and said to him, 'Rabbi, we know that you are a teacher who has come from God; for no one can do these signs that you do apart from the presence of God.' Jesus answered him, 'Very truly, I tell you, no one can see the kingdom of God without being born from above.' Nicodemus said to him, 'How can anyone be born after having grown old? Can one enter a second time into the mother's womb and be born?' Jesus answered, 'Very truly, I tell you, no one can enter the kingdom of God without being born of water and Spirit. What is born of the flesh is flesh, and what is born of the Spirit is spirit. Do not be astonished that I said to you, "You must be born from above." The wind blows where it chooses, and you hear the sound of it, but you do not know where it comes from or where it goes. So it is with everyone who is born of the Spirit.' Nicodemus said to him, 'How can these things be?' Jesus answered him, 'Are you a teacher of Israel, and yet you do not understand these things? Very truly, I tell you, we speak of what we know and testify to what we have seen; yet you do not receive our testimony. If I have told you about earthly things

and you do not believe, how can you believe if I tell you about heavenly things? No one has ascended into heaven except the one who descended from heaven, the Son of Man. And just as Moses lifted up the serpent in the wilderness, so must the Son of Man be lifted up, that whoever believes in him may have eternal life. For God so loved the world that he gave his only Son, so that everyone who believes in him may not perish but may have eternal life. Indeed, God did not send the Son into the world to condemn the world, but in order that the world might be saved through him. (John 3:1—17 NRSV)

The story of the visit of Nicodemus to Jesus in the third chapter of the Gospel of John, provides an instructive case study of the complex dynamics whereby the choice of being a slave in solidarity with a new community can become the means of transforming traditional human relationships and structures.

Nicodemus is a 'Master' in Israel. A person of recognised status and authority. One whose role and wisdom provided oversight and supervision for others. He assumes from the current talk about Jesus, and the use of terms such as the Lord, that He too is a Master. Yet Nicodemus chooses to come to see Jesus by night, indicating a hierarchy of 'Mastership', and placing that of Jesus in the mystery of darkness, rather than engaging as an equal in the mutuality of light that enables clarity of understanding and operation.

Nicodemus treats Jesus as a Master, from whom he can learn, someone overseeing a community and mediating knowledge. But he seeks to understand in literal terms and lacks the imagination and subtlety to recognise the creative notion of new birth. For Nicodemus 'Mastership' is to be expressed through discernible power and its measurable manifestations. He has little appreciation of an inner light which might struggle to illuminate worldly darknesses, yet be more deeply connected to the power and purpose of life. He thinks of rebirth as re-entering the maternal womb. Rebirth through water and the spirit invites a radically different perspective. Not growth from seed to fulfilment, but a continuing refinement to enable a better handling of the ongoing tension between darkness and light, between mortality and eternity.

A Downward Process

Jesus invites Nicodemus to explore the process, not to learn an answer. And the exploration is from weakness and dependence on God as the only Master. The call is to a faith which is constantly willing to be challenged and changed, to grow into a committed service of the Master and His agenda, explored through so many signs in St John's Gospel. For instance at the wedding in Cana, it is the slaves who do what is necessary to transform tragedy into glory. This is the faithful, unquestioning service of slaves to their Master: an early expression of discipleship. The call and the signs are given, the challenge is to listen, notice and obey, and to include others by serving them first.

Wisdom lies not in captured knowledge, but in spiritual discernment issuing from a prior stance of self-sacrificing service. The outcome is the creation of a new community, celebrating everyday life through this particular form of obedient ministry.

This mystery is explored more fully in chapter 6 of St John's Gospel, with the call to consume the Master – as the Bread of Life. Grace through everyday means, framed and offered by those whose service enables such a unique offer to be made, an offer beyond the canons of established religious practice or teaching.

The Master operates through offering a form of slave -like ministry and obedience to the will of the Father. In the garden of Gethsemane He makes this decision and commitment – not my will, but thy will be done.

The problem for Nicodemus was to recognise that just as God comes down to His struggling children, rather than the traditional religious programme of adherents progressing upwards towards the Divine, so those called into discipleship are invited to embrace this downward path. The call is to be with those at their points of real need, not to teach answers which provide understanding, but to offer solidarity that includes a primary willingness to go the extra mile – for the sake of serving better the needs of the other, and thereby creating a new solidarity.

Equal in Grace and Promise

Nicodemus is faced with a set of clear choices, about his desire, the desire of God, and the ways of seeking salvation for those who are suffering, as the gateway to the more inclusive glory of the kingdom. This is a call which invites every member of the Household, through a mutuality practised in prayer and sacraments, to participate in a gracious offer to all who might wish to receive it. Nicodemus the Master was invited to assume the calling of a slave in this context. And although he had a secret sympathy with this calling, he was unable to act publicly.

Pilate faced a similar dilemma in trying to use the title King to describe Jesus. The Messiah exercised His ministry not through force or competition, but from the cross. Through being arrested, tortured, killed as a slave who was perceived to be challenging the universally established systems of Mastery.

His followers were united in a Body, and all dedicated to serving the Head. This was de-privation in worldly terms, and a kind of Household in which hierarchy or right ordering according to Divine principles made every member equal as a slave to the Master. Even the apparently unseemly elements, as St Paul was to recognise, had a crucial part to play, one that was often underestimated.

Hence the emphasis which Jesus places throughout His ministry in identifying the hidden voices of those who were oppressed, exploited and suffering. This was the true meaning of Passover, when those who knew that they were slaves, were called to flee from earthly masterships into a new land of promise. This tradition finds an echo in John 12:2 where Jesus proclaims that if anyone serves me (slave), let that person follow me, i.e. the slave who came to serve is joined in the greater endeavour of the Master and His Household.

This is the basis of the radical unity proclaimed in John 17, that all followers may be one, in the service of the Father, in the way of the Son (slave), through the power of the Spirit of sacrifice and service.

Such a solidarity in service will arouse the hostility and hatred of a self-seeking world. The choice between slavery to self and slavery in Christ remains critical and continues throughout life in a fallen world where temptation ever arises to put self first. Hence the call to be a slave is a call to active service, through which grace is offered and enabled.

As for Nicodemus, so the notion of Master more widely was gender bound. Women were excluded and often exploited, and yet were equally opened to the call of the Christ for ministering God's grace through the service of need and anxiety. As this key theme within the New Testament is more clearly recognised, the contrast with the continuing preponderance of exploitation of women and children becomes more challenging. This fact needs more careful pursuit, both in the fight against modern slavery, and in the understanding of discipleship and its appropriate ways of being made manifest.

At the heart of this challenging call was the radical doctrine of the forgiveness of sin. A common process enabling light to be drawn out of darkness, liberating slaves to self and the idolatry of Mastership, in order to seek a downward trajectory towards the lowest place, from which grace is especially able to flow. This mystery has important implications for institutional as well as for individual life. Focused in the command in John 13:34—35 to love one another, or in the Johannine Epistles with the observation that one who does not love the brother or sister cannot know the love of God.

As Jesus states quite boldly in John 12:26 "if anyone serves me, let that person follow me: and where I am there will be my servant also". Similarly at the Last Supper Jesus is clear that the sign of the washing of the feet is the action of the Master becoming the slave as a model of the true discipleship, which creates a new community.

Those who seek to understand and unfold the Christian gospel in the perspective of the Enlightenment have tended to presuppose paradigms predicated on the primary importance of freedom. The call to discover self and identity by being freed from the constraints of darkness and sin. This important perspective can obscure the foundational emphasis in Christian calling upon the first step being a downward journey to more self-conscious and self-sacrificial service of God and neighbour.

The call to own the identity of the slave. "Not my will, but thy will be done". St Paul explores a similar reversal of priorities by highlighting the importance of the fact that "God chose the lowly things of this world and the despised things – and the things that are not." (1 Corinthians 1:28).

Such a starting perspective is in total contrast to those spiritualities which help to drive the market mechanisms and ideologies of the modern world, through which enslavement grows as a result of economic and social forces, including human greed and criminality. The foundation of the Gospel of Jesus the Christ, as Nicodemus was challenged to acknowledge, lies in the opposite of 'human   mastery'.

Just as Nicodemus struggled to understand this counterintuitive teaching and invitation, which seemed to be contrary to religious and political systems of human wisdom, so there is a temptation for the current Christian witness to avoid such challenging complexities and to rush straight towards the outcomes of slave -like service – the provision of support, security and comfort, with little interference with the disciples own mastery of their calling and its outworking.

The Gospel of Self-Fulfilment

The positive gospel of self-fulfilment has grown through a number of manifestations, such as being an expression of the political struggle for individual rights, the economic struggle for personal well-being, and the psychological concern for wholeness through guided reflection and increased self-confidence. Historical examples would be movements such as Christian socialism, the amazing growth of Christian charitable contributions, and the evolving of spiritualities of personal growth.

Such missionary strategies bear quick fruit because they can speak to people in the terms and values of their contemporary societies. The strategy has very little prophetic content or impact, though sometimes more radical possibilities might emerge through minority voices on the edge of mainstream mission and ecclesial models.

Forgiveness becomes a therapy for personal identity and can barely be recognised as a public element of the human story, except in extreme and very broad-based cases.

New models of human being are developed within existing paradigms of behaviour and organisation. The emphasis focuses upon progress, measured by outcomes as in much of the market ecology.

This complicity with contemporary values and approaches undermines the formative power of the cross: of the challenge "I, if I be lifted up, will draw all people to myself". Be lifted up in the public space as a slave deserving of death for undermining the basic presuppositions of religious and political cultures bases the gospel of the Christ upon the most radical prophetic act, with a defiant call to resistance, and a repentance or turning round which will enable the offering of a better way: the hodos (way) offered in Jesus of Nazareth.

It is this disjunction which highlights the important role and perspective of the victim. The slave is always a victim of current values and practices. The response can be a desire to escape and assume a place in the established power systems, which work through exploitation and exclusion. Or, a more humble commitment to use such a role to be an agent of the service which can engender love and open our eyes to new possibilities. This is the path of prophecy, shaped and pursued through the witness of the victim, which begins by exposing the brutality of unredeemed human societies, and bears the cost of the inevitable conflict and friction as seed or salt struggles to become effective in the attempt to nourish the wider world.

A Spirituality of Sacrifice

The element of victimhood ensures the focus of spirituality needing to be on the cross, and reinforced through sacraments of cleansing, fraction and being remade. This journey will take place through acknowledging affronts to human dignity and working through setbacks as well as signs of encouragement. Within this ecology of struggle it can become possible for those not formally in slavery to glimpse the mysterious powers of this journeying towards wholeness through brokenness, and to seek the lowest place of service for themselves. To grasp the significance of the invitation for the first to be last, so that the last may be first. Power subverted by powerlessness. A spirituality of giving oneself totally to the Master, for the working of His harvesting.

In this approach social justice no longer concentrates upon freedom as enshrined in equal rights or other deceptively seductive rhetorical moves. Instead justice for the social will emerge through moments and movements of service within established structures of unfreedom, providing different perspectives and possibilities, often expressed through what can appear to be unconnected strands and contradictions.

As Josephine Butler wrote in 1868 "education was what the slave owners most dreaded for their slaves, for they knew it to be the sure way to emancipation".[1] Social justice is always a process of enlightenment, much dependent upon the energy and insights of those living at the sharp end of societies evil dysfunctions and selfish exclusions.

Working with the leaders, institutions and perpetrators of exploitation, the role of the slave and victim is to enable the discernment of possibilities which can undermine the systematic dis-empowering of others, by addressing ways of richer participation. The aim will not be the award of rights as an abstract achievement (ironically already achieved in the twentieth century through the United Nations declarations) but a careful repairing of the torn fabric of social and political arrangements. There is always a need to create cultural space within which the path towards emancipation can be unfolded, in politics, in social systems, as in religious doctrines and practices.

Just as Jesus was willing to engage with Nicodemus, so the spirituality of slavery in His disciples needs to risk dialogue, alongside the demonstration of different practices and values. It was central that the Gospel emancipation of individuals was always enabled as part of a bold kingdom agenda for all structures and systems of exploitation and oppression.

The Beatitudes provide a powerful example of empowerment which can be both personal and political. The continuing temptation of organised religion is to shift a spirituality of slave like service which has prophetic intentions to enable radical reversals of power and much more inclusive participation, into a gentle expression of appreciative dependencies within existing structures. Service to what is already firmly established, in the way of the wisdom and Mastery represented by Nicodemus, rather than a devastatingly moving witness to the life changing powers of love, expressed through repentance, forgiveness and a new solidarity worked out through the Household of faith.

Confession and Conformity

Organised religion should always beware of the honoured place society accords to the mastery of Nicodemus: a force for stability, conformity and controlling frameworks designed to produce a more immediate version of a common good. It is important to examine this temptation, and to seek guidance for a more radically prophetic discipleship. This will be found in making a serious attempt to inhabit the discipline of confession and absolution as citizens, as a tester and transformer of social and political arrangements. Such a discipline is a key first stage in becoming properly prepared to share with others in the feast of the Master who took a towel and fulfilled the role of the slave in washing the feet of others: a process even more radically enacted in the breaking of the bread of His body and the shedding of His blood, to bring better news to others.

As both of these definitive actions make clear, the core is not to undertake a detailed analysis of the whole situation, nor to offer direct confrontation. The way of witness is more subtle, the giving of a sense of direction, the creation of a mood of wonder and gratitude (the true giving of self), and willingness to give the most basic service to others. All of these elements give immediate priority to goodness, not as a perfect ideal, but as a readily available experience which emerges through a sharing of activity in which one party willingly displays humility and weakness – a turning upside down of the normal power relationships to which human beings are tempted to be drawn. Thus a different set of attitudes and expectations can be created, not by the superior intellectual understanding and ministry of Nicodemus, but through the slave like actions of one who His followers too often tried to identify as Master in a traditional manner. Hence their appeal to command angels to fast forward His purposes.

New Life in Friendship

Such an approach changes the rules of the game, especially through the slaves' willingness to absorb injustice (the way of the cross), not through great schemes, but in countless small situations. Hence the eternal significance of every act of such discipleship. A radical democratisation of contributions which should frame understandings of the roles and structures inevitably developed to enable religious institutions and household to have any kind of organised existence.

This prophetic ministry creates new facts of experience, ones which are often ignored or unseen by commentators and analysts. These facts are pregnant with the power of grace and live through mood and imagination. Thus the worship of the Household must always be open to inspiration not simply through creeds and established liturgies, but also, and always, through a mutual sharing in this mood and imagination whereby grace is received with a thanks that empowers new possibilities for goodness, especially for a common good.

Jesus invited Nicodemus to be born again, through water and the spirit, the new facts of grace given, received and pushing for further goodness. A way of un-power which the slave incarnates most fully, cutting across the binaries of good and evil, master and slave, to create new possibilities through a radical generosity of spirit, which becomes the energy of new life for all who can become touched by it. Such is the power of what Marion terms un-power.

Albert Mason expresses this challenge succinctly "reality itself needs to be forgiven, because it cannot possibly live up to our delusional expectations".[2]

Thus the need of a totally self-giving love, which creates an agenda not for the self, but always for the other. The de-centring of self is the special witness of the slave – victim, not to collude with established structures and values, but to expose a totally different prospect for imagination and alternative action. With the self-de-centred (as in the challenge to Nicodemus) the centre can be reimagined by the combining of a variety of perspectives and aspirations, away from false ideals of equality as fair exchange, because real love looks for a deeper response of mutual service. Jesus tells His disciples that they are to be His friends. A relationship not subject to negotiation, but assumed and able to absorb difference and asymmetry. The Christian household is a forming and nourishing ground of such friendship.

Jesus offered Nicodemus friendship of this kind. The issue remains open as to how he really responded to this challenge to step away from the illusory securities of Mastership into the unknowable arenas of friendship. This ambiguity is significant because it highlights something about the essential intimacy which such slave like service can enable. The illusion of self-control can be given into a different kind of goal and identity. That of the slave fulfilling the role which is the key to opening the way to salvation.

Endnotes

[1] Josephine Butler. *The Education and Employment of Women*. Macmillan 1868, p16.

[2] Ed. H.de Vries and Nils F Schott. *Love And Forgiveness For a More Just World*. Columbia U.P. 2015, p20.

Questions For Further Reflection
And Group Discussion

1. *How might institutions, such as local churches, seek the lowest place?*

2. *What are the signs of engaging on the downward journey that Nicodemus was challenged to accept? Identify some marks of "the way of unpower".*

3. *What are the most urgent repairs needed to the torn fabric of our social and political arrangements?*

4. *How can friendship provide new resources for systems and strategies.*

CHAPTER - 8

St Paul and
the New Household of Faith

Domestic and Inclusive

Just as Jesus visited and stayed with families, and offered ministry from such a domestic setting, in the same way St Paul oversaw the development of the early church through Households. This was in line with the Jewish emphasis upon the Household as a site of worship and good practice. But the emerging church did not found the equivalent of synagogues and a Temple to be places for more public spirituality and formation. Rather, churches as discrete centres developed from Households. The ecclesia was formed and shaped in this domestic setting, providing a model of mixed participants and interchange between the personal and the public which all subsequent churches have been rooted within.

This means that a diverse, inclusive, mutually committed grouping made up an ecclesia. Differences brought together in the prayers and the breaking of the bread. There was a family feel to these communities, honouring the formation of family in Christ at the foot of the cross when Jesus says to people formally unrelated – behold your son, your mother.

Thus St Paul's letters pay special attention to family living, the complexities of diversity, and the disjunction between cultures rooted in oppressive hierarchy, whether Jewish, Greek or Roman, and this new way of being 'in Christ' together, whatever the hinterland of culture or context. From the beginning, the conversion of whole households ensured huge diversity of experience, expectation and operation. The small-scale made the model transferable into different locations, and equipped each 'church' with the sensitivities to be aware of the same dynamics of difference arising between churches, as well as within them.

Of course there were attempts to simplify and systematise 'church', often as part of power dynamics between different individuals and groups. Paul invested a great deal in trying to help Households work harmoniously in themselves, and in relation to others, as his letters to the Corinthians and the Galatians illustrate in vivid terms.

But the mission that could lead to the formation of a Christian Household generally took place in public locations, through engagement with live issues and challenges. In these encounters, apostles had wisdom and example to offer, including the narrative of salvation, and also much to learn about that particular place and the personnel involved. Questions which involve and engage are as important as statements and stories to share what Christians have been privileged to learn thus far.

The basic strategy was that of networking, supported by hospitality, interchange and common funding campaigns, to reach out to the most vulnerable. As Households attracted others, the doors would be opened to embrace a wider fellowship and set of concerns – a partnership in the gospel call to goodness and its active manifestation, especially in response to human need and vulnerabilities.

Reaching Down to be Raised Up

The whole church is described as "the Household of God" in 1 Corinthians 11; 1 Timothy 3:15 and 2 Timothy 2:20. The leader became "God's household manager" (Titus 1:7). A key part of this role of oversight was to ensure that the focus of the Household was not a simple reflection of the heathen practices of gathering to be raised up to God through rituals and prayers. Rather, the amazing good news of the Christian gospel was that God comes down to His children, into hearts, where two or three are gathered together, in the breaking of bread and in the sharing of the Word. Christian prayer and practice unfolded in this context of a real Presence, a power that gives confidence to own and confess weakness and failing and to reach out to others not in the strengths of those in the ecclesia, but through the power and mercy of God – indwelling, informing, inspiring, enabling – despite the honest confession of continuing failure and self-centredness, what Paul calls the temptation to fall into slavery to sin.

This peculiarly Christian experience of living in the presence of God issued into a being 'in Christ' that made Him present in encounters and challenges, both within the assembly, and as part of the work and witness of its members. Thus the offering of discipleship was an offering of the Master, through slaves seeking to be obedient, to any who would receive grace and goodness.

Nonetheless, there was often a response of hostility and suspicion, as evidenced by the persecution at Philippi (Philippians 1:30; 1 Thessalonians 2:2).

Amidst these blessings and challenges, there was the inevitable, and important, tendency to clarify teaching, practices and ways of decision-making. The danger became retreat into defended spaces, rather than the Gospel working through the vulnerabilities of encounter with the needs of others, within and without the Household. It is always the agenda of the other, the brother or sister unnoticed in the gutter as most people busily concentrate upon their own journeys, which provides the key inclusion of God's deeper presence, to be encountered through response and thus the material for reflection about longer term provision for enabling care and compassion to continue a common participation in the mercy and grace which alone brings salvation.

Each household needs to balance the demands of its own coherence and sustainability, with the enabling of encounter with those hidden but suffering expressions of God's most concentrated presence. Without such engagement there will be no proper nourishment through any existing provision of word, sacrament and fellowship. The demands of social justice are always to be sought out, responded to and reflected upon. Such a discipline ensures that the doors of the Household remain open to God's fuller presence. In this way discipleship thrives through the going out and coming in which enriches all family life.

In a society where the plurality of the public square makes it very difficult to notice and evaluate 'outside' patterns and practices, there needs to be a huge priority given to the missionary activity of going out, not necessarily to bring others into that particular Household (though the invitation is always open when appropriate) but rather so as to encounter God's presence and through acknowledging oneness in Christ with those who share

His vulnerability, there can be a nourishing of discipleship for Household members, and a scattering of seeds of mercy and grace in a manner that only God can bless.

Breaching The Walls Of Oppression

The discipline of letting go through sacrificial, slave -like service, becomes as important as the discipline of going out to engage and offer what seems to have already been established.

This larger landscape requires an astute awareness of the forces and cultures which allow or encourage crippling vulnerabilities. Archbishop Oscar Romero identified three broad streams:

- The idolatry of wealth
- The idolatry of national security
- The idolatry of the organisation[1]

The results of such prioritisation tended to find expression in the building of walls to ensure self-survival, self-security and self-control, all strategies which serve to exclude and marginalise others.

Besides providing an important framework for trying to understand the causes of oppression and the best ways of crafting appropriate responses, this kind of analysis highlights the importance of the Household of the ecclesia providing more wholesome models of sharing wealth, opening borders and establishing organisation that can bless the needy and the stranger. Pope Paul VI called for "a civilisation of love".[2] The Christian Household has a key role in this structuring of a kingdom presence. Thus each Household has a public and a political task.

The tools are a commitment with St Paul to show no partiality, to privilege the vulnerable, to model an open table fellowship, and to challenge narrow self- defensive border construction. The method is that of sacrifice, which owns fallibility and failure, trusts in forgiveness, and has faith in the visitation that is offered in the poor and needy. This presents a huge challenge to the growing tribalisms of the twenty-first century: it presents an urgent missionary task.

The style will not be to point or shout at others, but to follow the One who made Himself a slave to serve others, even amidst all the complex and competing selfishness of his disciples.

Presence In The Poorest

Hence the importance of reflection, within the household around word, sacrament and fellowship in a common life, but also in relation to the search which privileges encounters beneath the systems and structures that so often create barriers and boundaries. Too often energy is concentrated too narrowly on this latter agenda of systems and structures, without receiving the wisdom from the presence of God discerned in the casualties and the marginalised.

The Household of the church has a particular vocation to pursue both of these outside agendas, but always through the perspective of the poorest. This allowed the church to appeal to conscience, and moral value, as the foundation and shaper of practice, and as a deeper critique in the refining of possible responses through missionary witness. The priority of the poor recognised so succinctly by Pusey, who sold personal possessions to build St Saviours Church to be a Christian Household in the needy town of nineteenth century Leeds.

The Household is not a contribution to a particularly systematic response to need. It simply highlights a range of coexisting pressures and possibilities and seeks partnership for response aimed at mercy and blessing for those being made most vulnerable. Especially in a society where few say "Blessed are the poor" because most would subscribe to the values "Happy are the rich".

Such a Household provides the essential space for discipleship to be nourished and expressed as witness. Paul was clear in Galatians 6:2—4: "Bear one another's burdens, and so fulfil the law of Christ... But let everyone prove their own work... For every person must bear their own burden".

The Household is a place to enable witness and outreach which encounters the Presence of God in ways which are essential to the proper flourishing of the church as the Body of Christ. At the same time it seeks to enable each disciple to take responsibility for their own particular calling and its expression. Again, there can be a danger of trying to resolve this important tension by drawing keen Christians into the organisational life of the church. This can become a form of idolatry, for the institution and for the individuals concerned.

Discipleship As Widening Sympathy

The effective witness of the individual disciple depends upon connection with others. Participation provokes a dynamic of interaction, from which participants and those in wider networks can benefit, and towards which they can contribute.

This reality is against what Edward Caird called "an insipid uniformity of thought and action in all the members". Rather the call is to be a Household in which "the utmost diversity of gift is used to manifest the same Spirit". Those who shut others out of their life, thereby shut themselves in. The key to a flourishing Household and a healthy discipleship is "that widening of sympathy which makes the life and interests of others part of one's own".[3]

Thus institutional life and individual vocation need to be structured to always enable this wider encounter and richer reflection. The response of dioceses and parishes to the Clewer Initiative call to reach out to those bound by modern slavery and other forms of abusive oppression, is an indicator of how this challenge can be recognised and responded to in our contemporary society. Each of us can be of more significance as a Christian, and as a citizen, in this calling to achieve our own fulfilment through our contribution to the flourishing of the greater whole.

This is Jesus's call in Mark 10:29—30 : "There is no one who has left house, brothers, sisters, father, mother, wife, children, lands, for my sake and the Gospels, who will not receive a hundredfold, now in this life, houses…….. With persecution, and in the world to come eternal life".

The vocation is now, "in this time", not just into eternity. And the fruits, including persecution, will be in real time, amidst real situations of engagement and challenge , always for His sake, thus, conforming to the kingdom agenda proclaimed in Luke 4 and summarised in Matthew 25, as measured through good news being experienced by those in need – the poor, the marginalised, the oppressed.

The way of the cross is not just a personal path, but always part of the corporate unfolding of the Gospel of Jesus Christ. It means that there can be no simple division between sacred and secular: between faith and knowledge: between religion and unbelief.

Caird said to his undergraduates in Balliol "The beginning of religious life is always such an awakening to the greatness that underlies the littleness of our ordinary experience".[4] This is our participation not just with others, but in the conflict being fought out between good and evil, in which we are all every day of our lives taking sides.

In this way "a greater divine purpose is being realised, to which, whether we will or not, we are always contributing". This explains the temptation of religion to define itself by withdrawal and separation, because of a perceived danger of contamination or temptation.

A Framework For Human Flourishing

For Christian discipleship the cross is the place of encounter with evil and temptation, by confrontation through the offer of a better way, not through retreat into a self-constructed safe space. Discipleship seeks redemption in the present, through fullest openness to the purifying Presence of God.

The Household is called to enable this pathway for individuals, by forming groups for all classes and conditions of people. An example would be the strategy of William Wilberforce. Nourished in his own domestic household, he found the ecclesial Household of his parish church to be the place for forming friendships and discerning the call of discipleship. Hence the Clapham sect. This classic parochial 'Household' gathered Christians for public worship, as a witness and an invitation within the community for which they willingly accepted pastoral responsibility. The group who gathered around Wilberforce met to pray, to read the Bible, and to seek to identify the implications of their Christian callings. They began with personal morality and integrity. Not as an end in themselves but as foundations from which to contribute to the wider society.

The challenge was to invite personal response from others, hence operations like the campaign for the Reform of Public Manners. But there was an equally clear recognition of the role of the state in providing a framework for human flourishing. Slavery was a contradiction of such an aspiration, and thus the state and public opinion needed to be encouraged to recognise the oppression of Slavery and to adjust the framework for human flourishing appropriately.

The Household of Faith practised an inclusive ministry in its own context yet recognised that some members would be called to share this graciousness into the wider society, into the Household of the nation. The way of discipleship could not be contained in a personal or even local journey. There were always greater implications to be recognised and pursued. The aim was "to come into obedience to the law of brotherhood... To those energies that, left to the law of nature, can produce only the struggle of existence, known to modern political economy under the name of free competition".[5] Within history Kaufman saw the journey of the household as a progression from association by compulsion, to association by contract, to association by communion. Interestingly, religious groups easily shift in the opposite direction, from communion, to contract, to compulsion.

The impersonal nature of huge issues and complex challenges needed to be alleviated by friendship and the practice of active virtues measured by their effect on the material improvement of the most vulnerable. Thus the Household becomes an interpretative community, in its own setting, yet always looking outwards. The measure is recognised to be outcomes and not mere aspirations. More demonstrable expressions of human flourishing, locally, nationally and internationally.

Endnotes

[1] R.M. Della Rocca. *Romero*. DLT 2015, p86.

[2] Pope Paul VI. *St Peter's Square*. Pentecost Sunday 1970.

[3] E. Caird. *Lay Sermons*. Maclehose 1907.

[4] Ibid.

[5] M. Kaufman. *Christian Socialism*. Kegan Paul 1888, p28.

Questions For Further Reflection And Group Discussion

1. *How can the Household of the church remain an open space for all in need, and not succumb to the temptation to give priority to its own identity and workings?*

2. *Identify some local examples of the visitation that is offered through Christ's presence in the poor and needy.*

3. *How can the way of the cross be not just a personal path, but always part of a corporate unfolding of the Gospel of Jesus Christ?*

4. *What can be learned from William Wilberforce about the movement from local to national witness?*

CHAPTER - 9

Slavery – The Ecclesial Vocation: An Anglican Response

The Dynamics Of Difference

The Church of England was born out of the fracturing of secure frameworks, and an urgent need to embrace diversity positively. Richard Hooker produced foundational theology based upon the doctrine of participation, as citizens and not simply as self-selected members of a particular religious organisation. The Gospel embraced the whole of life and the church was called to serve a kingdom project. Images such as the Vine in John 15 and the Body in 1 Corinthians 12 provided models of a living inclusivity which served to provide for different parts, fed by a common life and overseen by a common Head. Diversity was presumed and embraced at the deepest levels of creation and the mutual flourishing recognised as salvation.

Thomas Cranmer captured something of this calling by establishing a Book of Common Prayer, for all seasons, locations and sorts of people. Sentences read before the collection of alms indicated the practical priority of a conjoining charity to enable a richer common life.

As the establishment provided more security and an official identity to enable a national dependency upon the Church of England, so the focus shifted to institutional well-being and effectiveness. Others were called to conform, rather than participate in the dynamics of difference being debated and negotiated through common prayer and a presumed common good.

By the nineteenth century, the industrial revolution had highlighted a massive fragmentation of society, socially, economically and culturally, with few means of connecting or negotiating across different experiences and perspectives. One response was an expansion of the conforming and combining role of government, and a variety of bids to provide a suitable overseeing religious framework – catholic, evangelical and liberal. In the midst of these forces forming and flexing their muscles so as to best contribute within existing power structures, E.B. Pusey, a Professor of Theology at Oxford, and a contributor towards the catholic type of response to the problem of division was prescient enough to recognise that the key model and marker for the gospel was the poor. In a sermon in the 1860s he said, "In our strivings for Christian life, right choices and disciplines, the key is to love God in His poor, where He is most especially present, as in the sacrament".[1]

Those in the most need, often hidden from plain sight, are the "witness of the continuing gift of Presence"[2] from which humanity can learn, be nourished and be embraced in a common mercy". He went on: "The poor have a secret character about them; they bring a blessing with them; for they are what Christ for our sake made Himself".[3] The poor were not be treated as a privileged category in themselves, but always as one element of a set of diverse ingredients from which grace and mercy can flow, through their interactions as a practical manifestation of the outworking of love.

Slavery: A Contemporary Testing

Modern slavery has become such a testing place in contemporary society, and challenges the involvement of all sectors, including victims, in discerning and responding to a common presence and a connecting promise.

The challenge becomes the call to rediscover and re-inhabit a living participation in a common good. In the twentieth century, in an age of the mass production of goods, services and ideas, socialism seemed to provide important clues, especially in the theology of Anglican teachers such as Henry Scott Holland and Charles Gore, both disciples of F.D. Maurice. Their work was given a clear expression for public implementation in the teaching of William Temple, with an emphasis upon middle axioms, providing a frame and guiding principles for interpreting God's call and purposes, and human response. Christians could assist in the identification and implementation of basic principles such as freedom, fellowship and service, but always sensitive to context.

The aim was to provide a frame for development, within which those in need could be identified and invited to be involved, but overseen by the authority of roles, analysis and experienced application. The issues were identified by William Beveridge in a report published in 1942, as five giants on the road of reconstruction...... Want, disease, ignorance, squalor and idleness.[4] The outcome was influential in the creation of what came to be known as the welfare state. Published during the Second World War, this report promised rewards for everyone's sacrifices.

The model remains an important and attractive one for those in power, providing tools for analysis, identifying helpful values, and appropriate involvement of those at the sharp end, the poor and oppressed.

With the post-modern suspicion of overarching assessment and solutions, and the dissolution of many of the traditional levers of power such as close government oversight or universally recognised religious teaching, the approach in the twenty-first century is beginning to focus not on mediating principles but on mediating practices. An echo of the theology of the Beatitudes where hearts meet beyond the usual classification around a deeper agenda of grace and commitment to the needs of the other. The disciple is no longer a servant of a particular legal or moral framework, with defined roles, responsibilities and contributions. Instead the disciple becomes the catalyst for giving at the point of need, often into very localised settings (as with the Good Samaritan), leading to work with others to evolve systems of care and response, and to allow this lived experience to inform ongoing attempts to create adequate policies and standard practices.

This is the service of the 'slave', dependent upon the needs of others and putting self totally and sacrificially into contributing to the needs of the most desperate, which will shape the tone, scale and practice being evolved. The model becomes the creation of appropriate Households for care and for the receiving of grace and mercy.

On The Way

This is the way of kenosis, not dependent on established institutions, whether of church, state, business or community, but the creation of new, mobile arrangements – a less stable, pop-up spirituality, an echo of Jesus always going on to the next village. Grace given and received "on the way".

One important ingredient is the view and the experience of the victim, so that commodification can be transformed into companionship. Thus for the Clewer Initiative current equivalents of Beveridge's five giants are to be discerned in more contemporary indications of the image of God being damaged:

- vulnerability;

- homelessness/migration and nowhere to lay the head/ inadequate accommodation;

- hidden exploitation;

- the denial of agency to enforce total dependency;

- being controlled by powerful systems organised for the benefit of others.

The key becomes not assessment to enable the best targeted responses within a measured framework such as the welfare state. Rather the approach is based upon the development of real projects in real time with people in damaging contexts, from which will emerge signs for strategy and policy. Of course these potential outcomes will always be subject to modification, because power emerges from the tasting of grace and mercy, not from human attempts to capture and administer such possibilities. A more contemporary manifestation of Hegel's dialectic breaking down established ways of knowing and doing, to allow new and more inclusive forms to be evolved – often by taking seriously the path of suffering.

This approach is important because more complete and systematic models fail to give proper priority to the reality of trauma and damage, and the need for a flexible, uneven rebuilding of resilience and more confident aspiration. In Mexico girls and women rescued from sex slavery are given a blank piece of paper on which to begin to rebuild their lives – not a manual for improvement and return to better health, but invitation to dream and be changed so as to step with confidence into the unknown.

The culture of such care is not about compliance but rather invites participation from all kinds of places and perspectives. Similarly values arise from this kind of cooperative collaboration, rather than from formulae and dogmatic teaching. To look into the eyes of the victim is to put a refining reality into every scheme of moral values.

Resistance

Such a bottom-up approach demands a lightness of touch at the centre, and policy which continually responds to good practice. It is especially relevant in a time of poly-criminality, a complexity about the nature of evidence for law enforcement and the operation of statutory agencies, and the huge need for intelligence and caring contributions from citizens and consumers.

There is an urgent need to build Households of resistance, across the Empires of exploitation and oppression, in which victims have a place and a role. We must beware the temptation to simply aim to build resilient communities, the emphasis must be on resistance and cultural change, not simply survival. Such a distinction changes the calling of all who contribute.

Households gathered in this manner will not focus on the poor as holding the key, in the way made popular by liberation theology. Rather there is a need for a Dionysian dynamic of participation through appropriately called and equipped orders, each serving others, and bound together through their common priestly mediating roles. The resulting interactions will provide a complex of contributions, held together in the greater dynamic of God's mercy and grace – a mutual probation which tests and approves morality and its expressions. Just as Christ's resurrection is an enactment of hope which completes itself through a process of mutual indwelling and corporate witness. This calling is captured in the invitation "feed my sheep".

Every soul accesses hope through sharing in this mutuality of mercy, something St Paul calls koinonia, that is participation in a certain kind of Household. The Gospel warns against false hopes and false gods, the aspirations of a particular perspective or experience, whether of victims or perpetrators or helpers. The common way of grace is tasted in the mutuality of action for the common goods of the kingdom, measured against the five indicators of the Gospel call.

Location And Direction

This means that the underlying agenda of any programme for such social justice, is that of location, each owning a degree of being a stranger, a pilgrim, on the way, embracing the challenges of hope deferred, success marred, failures fuelled in defeat and disappointment, and yet trusting in the way of the cross as the way of justice which brings eternal salvation, the coming of the kingdom, through the visiting realities of suffering, struggle and imperfection. The primacy of location places the parish at the centre of possible responses and co-actions.

Discipleship is following this uncertain way, nourished by the signs of Presence, especially manifest in human need and suffering, and tasted in receiving grace together. The prevalent power of sin, or falling short, requires the rooting of this response in confession, personal and corporate: always open to owning new complicity in the forces of oppression, and yet receiving new mercy. JB Mozley in a university sermon noticed how "the Pharisees converted their conscience into a manageable compassion".[5] This easily becomes the path of false discipleship.

Hence the importance of spaces for intimate sharing, mutual criticism and the testing of mutuality. Besides public worship, there is an increasing need for Households of reflection and mutual support around the agenda of noticing, responding and thus receiving – through the act of engagement and sacrificial service. Such partnerships will always be partial and unfinished places of contribution and reception, needing to value signs and moments, rather than schemes and systems.

The call of discipleship is to a sense of direction, participating with others, but always open to new challenges and possibilities. Amongst the huge variety of opportunities around slavery/vulnerability; homelessness/immigration/ inadequate accommodation; hidden exploitation; the denial of agency; being controlled by powerful systems organised for the benefit of others - there has to be courage to accept a call to the particular, in what might seem like a narrow space, while trusting the power of grace to overflow in other areas without our own involvement or understanding. The way is a journey of faith, marked by real engagement, not generalities and overarching schemes which satisfy the desire for order and control, but often fail to deliver effective relief to the real points of suffering and abuse.

Households of Faith: Purposeful Parishes

Such faith Households will be agents of justice, alongside other participants – not the controlling model of Christendom, but an exercise in comradeship and cooperation. These kinds of models will reflect the sheer diversity and complexity of an Anglican polity expressed through parishes.[6] Localised centres of identity and engagement, taking seriously the realities and limitation of human lives being placed within the difficult dynamics of imbalanced and exploitative power relationships, an ever present sense of a lack of resources, and a bewildering array of inter-activities with the wider world. Within such settings there is great value in a contextualised response, consciously committed to being part of the widest possible endeavour for the flourishing of all creatures within the whole of creation. This model owns the importance of concentrating the small resources of salt, leaven, light or seeds, that will seem to be available in any particular setting, so that energy, synergy, new models and hopeful signs can be crafted as appropriate. The laboratory of concentrated commitment endeavouring to connect creatively with realising the greater potential for mutual human flourishing that human hearts are capable of glimpsing and pursuing, once the powerfully narrow focusing of the market massaging each self is put into a proper perspective.

Each small local outpost can become a contributor to growing greater wholeness, for participants, for particular contexts and challenges, and for the globalising way of owning a common calling and journeying. The enduring qualities of the parish system offer important resources in terms of an absolute inclusivity of aspiration, maximising offering of service, and a focused, deepening of commitment and crafting of ways of witness, invitation and co-working for the fulfilment of creation. The Spirit enabling the wholeness that is the beginning, earthly stage, of the growing of that holiness within which God becomes ever more fully present and purposeful.

Endnotes

[1] E.P. Pusey. *Parochial Sermons*. Rivingtons 1873, Vol.1, p26.

[2] Ibid, p60.

[3] Ibid, p74.

[4] William Beveridge. *Social Insurance and Allied Services*. 1942.

[5] J.B. Mozley. *Sermons Preached Before The University of Oxford*. Rivingtons 1877, p40.

[6] Alastair Redfern. *The Word on the Street*. ISPCK 2015.

Questions For Further Reflection And Group Discussion

1. *William Beveridge, in 1942, identified five key issues: want, disease, ignorance, squalor and idleness. What would be the equivalent challenges today?*

2. *Take a blank piece of paper and make signs of your dreams for the future. How would they relate to women and girls rescued from a sex slavery?*

3. *What would be the features of Households of Resistance?*

4. *How can a local church become "a laboratory of concentrated commitment"?*

PART FIVE
Discipleship and Mission

CHAPTER - 10

The Spirituality of The Slave Disciple

Sharing In Paying The Cost

Much Christian teaching recognises that God is known most deeply in human vulnerability. As expressed in Psalm 19:2 "night to night declares knowledge". This is the message articulated in the Beatitudes, and by Paul's honesty about meeting God in his weakness. Dependency is a key element of acknowledging our creatureliness, and our need of God and of others. The doctrines and teachings of the church can help to enable recognition of this important truth about human being, but the reality is met most clearly in the living out of vulnerability with others as the unfolding of an earthly journey.

Hence the vital role of ecclesial communities, or Households, within which such dependency can be accepted and blessed. Thus establishing an alternative narrative to the worldly attempts to build systems of self-sustaining strength. Growth in the spiritual life is through the struggle to own our need of others and our need of God. In the parable of the sheep and goats in Matthew 25:31—46 there is a crucial dynamic between contemplation-

"we see you" and targeted action: "feeding, visiting, and caring". The discipline of contemplation projects beyond the immediate needs of the self and defines significant acting in the world through seeing with the eyes of those in most need.

This is a slave spirituality. Giving priority to the Master and His agenda: that is, the well-being and inclusion of His children who are most in need because of being neglected and exploited. The expression of this spirituality and its outcomes will be a witness to the ways of the Master, not any kind of achievement of the disciple. The aim is not the nourishment of the disciple, but a redistribution of power, through the disciple being willing to contribute to the cost involved. This is the stance of a self-sacrificing service of others, especially into the structures which oppress, as well as the caring for those who are suffering. The Eucharist provides the model and critique for all systems of organising human relationships and learning how to inhabit them most effectively.

This calling is grounded in the miracle of being able to lose the self in order to be "in Christ". In his commentary on the Epistle to the Galatian (1535), Luther wrote:

> "God sent his only begotten Son into the world and laid upon him all the sins of all men, saying be thou Peter, that denier; Paul, that persecutor, blasphemer and doer of violence; David, that adulterer; that sinner who ate the apple in Paradise; that thief on the cross – in the sum, be thou the person who committed the sins of all men".[1]

Christ is the Messiah in this space of universal crucifixion: the slave of all enslaved to sin, who nonetheless through Him, can turn around and themselves respond to the call to become agents of this Ministry of salvation. For example, it was after the last supper that Peter denied Jesus, long after his ministerial commission to be a founding element of the church, and yet he could be forgiven and recommissioned by the risen Lord.

This is a process and a miracle beyond human understanding, because it is not simply incremental or expressible in formulae and established practices. Paul recognised this mystery in 1 Corinthians 2:9, "eye has not seen, nor ear heard, neither have entered into the heart of man, the things which God has prepared for those that love Him". Such love is a total self-giving, in response to the call and generosity of the Master. There is always a danger that the disciple tries to capture this experience of grace in ways that create a system of morality, so that the initiative and authority rest in human constructs, rather than in living service to the mystery of love ever flowing from the Master to embrace slaves in our sinfulness. The foundational truth of the Gospel which Luther grasped so clearly.

A Living Relationship

In the Christian life the relationship of Master and slave can never be captured in a legal framework. It is a living relationship rooted in grace as an active, overflowing force of generous goodness. Such grace continually overcomes law and enables the continuing recognition of those being exploited and excluded, because of the limitations of the law and the inward -looking tendencies of human arrangements translated into various forms of mastery. In Romans 4:15 Paul dramatically declares, that "the law worketh wrath".

Clearly human society needs law, systems and structures of oversight, and many Christians are called to enable these important elements, but each calling is to be rooted in a deeper call to be a slave of the One Master, and thus to bear witness to the penultimacy of all such activities, since they require a continual subjection to the refining and confession of failings in order to be ever open to new challenges and necessities on behalf of those most damaged or disadvantaged by any current arrangements. In every Christian calling there is an element in each disciple which remains Peter the betrayer or Paul the persecutor, taking bearings from more immediate markers, and neglecting the discipline of contemplation of the needs of the un-noticed, through which God's recommissioning continually takes place.

What is true for discipleship comes through obedience rather than through the human freedoms which have come to dominate Western liberal societies. Abraham was called to go to a place he did not know, in order to participate through dependence on others. Echoes of "My God why have you forsaken me?" – the cry from a dying slave. This is a way of anxiety, not a cosy dependence of a child in her mother's arms, which too easily becomes the preferred model for Christian spirituality.

Rather there is need to face the challenge of accepting the sign of being adopted, into a context which in many ways will be strange and alien, yet a place where love can embrace, involve and transform. A love we can never capture or control, a love which can only be received, for healing, hope and empowering into the dynamic service which brings transformation to those most in need of these qualities.

See : Judge : Act

This means that in an important sense Christian life does not flow from worship services and private prayer. This would be a reflection of some contemporary attempts to capture mission in the sequence, See-Judge-Act. The presupposition is that a person is converted/nourished by Scripture, sacraments and testimony in order to purify and refine judgement about themselves and their context, so that they can effectively and faithfully act out the Christian life – having been formed better in Christ's image to do His work.

Such a sequence holds important insights, but it easily reduces into a power structure whereby the church, the ministry, and traditions of teaching and praying, become definitive. The result is that discipleship becomes an obedient response to 'church' in order to replicate that power dynamic towards others – making them an offer to enable them to be similarly transformed and equally dependent upon what 'church' offers or decrees.

Act : Judge : See

In fact the Gospel of Jesus Christ, in His own ministry, and in that of the disciple most formative for the church, the apostle Paul, operated through the opposite sequence. The good news began in people's lives with encounter – an action of God through others. Even St Paul's more direct mystical encounter with Jesus needed to be completed and confirmed by his encounter with Ananias. Encounter is the action of God through the lives of others, leading to judgement in the soul enabling a new 'seeing'. The Gospel works by allowing the blind to see. The paradigmatic witness is the man born blind with his constant refrain "I was blind, now I can see", as a result of a real encounter with new life in Jesus Christ.

This is the missionary opportunity unfolding through the ministry around modern slavery. Many people of goodwill, often having little formal knowledge or contact with the church, are moved to join in the endeavours to combat this wicked crime. People are moved by encountering the plight of the victims, the imperfections and cruelty of human systems, and the generosity and commitment of so many who have become involved in this cause – both voluntary and statutory contributions. From this experience of encounter with the fact of slavery and victimhood, comes a spiritual movement, a desire to sacrifice self, in order to become a slave to serve the needs of victims and would-be restorers and rescuers of the victims. A desire to contribute toward the reform and improvement of systems and values.

The experience of acting opens, develops and focuses this spiritual movement so that judgement becomes more generous, more critical of criminality and failing systems, and more hopeful of the potential which can flow from communion amongst believers in this cause. Partnerships spring up which are Households of committed actors, longing to include the excluded and the oppressed in a mutual fellowship and nourishing friendship. What St Paul would term Koinonia.

The fight against slavery flows through these small gatherings of committed disciples at every level, often drawing together an amazing variety of people and perspectives. The sequence which develops such effective discipleship for the coming of the kingdom is Act-Judge-See. This sequence is enabling people to experience, interpret and see themselves and the world which we inhabit in a new way. A way which is committed to recognising exclusion (Luke 4 and Matthew 25 – the book ends of Jesus's Gospel), and which responds by finding ways to reach out to victims: "Come to me all who labour and are heavily burdened" and to challenge corrupting systems and immoral, selfish values.

Owning Sin Opens Salvation

The intriguing challenge for the church, is how to recognise and celebrate this kingdom approach to discipleship, so resonant of the New Testament, so as to enable proper flourishing and development and recognise the importance of space to reflect upon what such contemporary movement might have to say to our current approach to mission. The hard challenge is to explore the extent to which our understanding and organisation of 'church' needs to be broken open, so that discipleship does not depend upon being converted into set practices, but rather becomes a radical engagement with the slaves of society, in the power of the Slave on the cross, to enable the love of God to flow more freely between His children and across creation

In an age when much of life, including the life of the church, is dominated by a trust in rationalism that produces systems always in need of refinement, it is worth noting the point made by Augustine, that God "did not wish a rational creature made in his own image to have Dominion save over irrational creatures: not man over man, but man over the beasts".[2] For Augustine the cause of slavery was not nature, but sin.

In a period when climate change is becoming an increasingly important agenda to unite rational people in recognising the challenge of assuming some responsibility for the planet, it is imperative that the gospel of Jesus Christ can deepen that movement of spirit to own the equally urgent need to recognise responsibilities for the well-being of fellow human being who are being exploited and destroyed in increasing numbers. Further, this Gospel calls not just for interest, but for a radical commitment, a serious self-giving for the sake of the other, i.e. the well-being of creatures and creation beyond the immediate self and its more obvious desires, choices and morality. A concern for children created and called for eternity.

Slavery to sin begins to assume a more recognisable currency, as it is manifested by the continuing crucifixion of the planet and of so many of its most vulnerable inhabitants. The passion narrative continues to be an indicator of the realities of human weaknesses and failings, but also impetus for hope, faith and the triumph of love. The way of discipleship is one of attunement with the spirit of grace through encountering the limitation and the cries for salvation that constitute the extremes of human being. Such encounters confront our experience, our assessment of that experience, and our visioning of what therefore might be our values and perspectives to inform further encounters.

Sin is acknowledged and hearts are opened to salvation through the forgiveness and dependency to which the Lord's prayer calls all who would follow Christ. A way continually unfolding not through the security of church, but through the struggles for community amidst the darkness of sin and evil.

The Passion Narrative Continues: Play A Part
The spirituality of discipleship calls for absolute obedience to God's agenda in the face of every testing encounter. The courage to put the needs of the most vulnerable and unnoticed first, and the wisdom to learn with others about better shaping values and community for the future.

This discipline provides the new frame not just for individuals, but for the Households in which each needs to find their nourishment and confirmation of calling.

As this process and spiritual unfolding occurs in diverse groupings ('Households') across the country in response to modern slavery, so we need to reflect upon what such practical and effective witness is contributing to a proper expression of the Gospel, and to consider what lessons this amazing phenomenon might have for the practice of 'church' amongst committed Christian people.

Social justice expressed through practice, rather than the formulation of principles from Christian sources to be applied to practice. In the encounter is enlightenment and the tasting of new life. The passion narrative continues, on the edge of conventional religious practice. The focus has always been outside the city wall on the boundaries of human systems of solidarity and control.

Our reflection upon the spirituality discernible in the response to modern slavery might encourage us to look beyond the frameworks which have served us well, but too easily reflect the ways and values of the self- protecting society. New ways will ever emerge in the encounter which occurs amidst the needs of God's children. Our Christian institutions exist to serve and enable that Gospel gracing process: Act-Judge-See. Encounter enables interpretation enlightened through the revelation emerging from the perspective of those hitherto hidden and victimised so that the disciple sees the self and others in a new way.

This is the method of mission by which discipleship and a faithful church are called, formed, inspired and enabled. The sending or missio from the presence of God in the cries of the hidden and exploited, which reveals new possibilities for the coming of the kingdom, and new paths of testimony and the creation of safe and saving communities.

Endnotes
[1] M. Luther. *Commentary on Galations*. CreateSpace 2014.

[2] P. Garnsey. *Ideas of Slavery from Aristotle to Augustine*. CUP 1996, p216.

Questions For Further Reflection
And Group Discussion

1. *In which ways can the parable of the sheep and goats in Matthew 25:31—46, be seen as a summary of the call to discipleship?*

2. *When we are guilty of betrayal or violence to others, how do we seek forgiveness and recommissioning in our discipleship?*

3. *How might the increasing concern about climate change and the well-being of the planet, be better aligned with the equally urgent need to confront the destruction of people through modern slavery?*

4. *The passion narrative continues "outside the city walls", beyond the marks of normal civilisation. What is our part in this ongoing narrative of passion — being done to for the sake of others, and as a gateway to eternal life?*

Epilogue

Do you not know that if you present yourselves to anyone as obedient slaves, you are slaves of the one whom you obey, either of sin, which leads to death, or of obedience, which leads to righteousness? But thanks be to God that you, having once been slaves of sin, have become obedient from the heart to the form of teaching to which you were entrusted, and that you, having been set free from sin, have become slaves of righteousness.

I am speaking in human terms because of your natural limitations. For just as you once presented your members as slaves to impurity and to greater and greater iniquity, so now present your members as slaves to righteousness for sanctification.

When you were slaves of sin, you were free in regard to righteousness.

So what advantage did you then get from the things of which you now are ashamed? The end of those things is death. But now that you have been freed from sin and enslaved to God, the advantage you get is sanctification. The end is eternal life. (Romans 6:16-22 NRSV).

For you were called to freedom, only do not use your freedom as an opportunity for self indulgence, but through love become slaves to one another. For the whole law is summed up in a single commandment, "you shall love your neighbour as yourself." (Galatians 5:13-14. NRSV).